"You have one hell of a nerve, butting in where you don't belong."

Jenny's back stiffened. "Abby is my student, and that gives me every right to offer assistance."

"Fine. Now, back off," Adam said.

"You are the most exasperating man!" Her narrowed eyes sparked with temper.

Damned if Adam didn't want to kiss her more than ever.

"This is your daughter we're talking about! Make. The. Time."

"Point taken." He pushed a strand of incredibly soft hair off her face, and tucked it behind her ear.

Awareness darkened her eyes. "What—what are you doing?" she asked.

Adam lost the fight to keep his distance. Stepping closer, he cupped her head between his hands. "Getting ready to kiss you."

Dear Reader,

This is the first book in my Saddlers Prairie miniseries, which takes place in Montana prairie country. Years ago, NPR aired a fascinating series on one-room schools across the United States. In one story, a teacher mentioned a little girl who didn't talk when she started kindergarten. The teacher saw a spark in the girl's eyes and knew she was smart. Through love and encouragement from the teacher and the entire class, the little girl did learn to speak. I have never forgotten this story, and decided to tell my own about Adam Dawson, a single rancher with a mute little girl about to enter kindergarten. Jenny Wyler is a teacher and new to town, with a few challenges of her own to face. I hope you enjoy Adam and Jenny's story as much as I enjoyed writing it.

I love to hear from readers. Contact me through my website, www.annroth.net, email me at ann@annroth.net, or write me at P.O. Box 25003, Seattle, WA 98165-1903. Also, please visit my website at www.annroth.net and enter the monthly drawing to win a free book! You'll also find my latest writing news and a monthly new, delicious recipe.

Happy reading!

Ann Roth

Rancher Daddy

ANN ROTH

TORONTO NEW YORK LONDON
AMSTERDAM PARIS SYDNEY HAMBURG
STOCKHOLM ATHENS TOKYO MILAN MADRID
PRAGUE WARSAW BUDAPEST AUCKLAND

In loving memory of my beloved mother,
Alice Caroline Berman Roth

Recycling programs
for this product may
not exist in your area.

ISBN-13: 978-0-373-75394-9

RANCHER DADDY

Copyright © 2012 by Ann Schuessler

ABOUT THE AUTHOR

Ann Roth lives in the greater Seattle area with her husband. After earning an MBA she worked as a banker and corporate trainer. She gave up the corporate life to write, and if they awarded PhDs in writing happily-ever-after stories, she'd surely have one.

Ann loves to hear from readers. You can write her at P.O. Box 25003, Seattle, WA 98165-1903 or email her at ann@annroth.net.

Books by Ann Roth

HARLEQUIN AMERICAN ROMANCE

1031—THE LAST TIME WE KISSED
1103—THE BABY INHERITANCE
1120—THE MAN SHE'LL MARRY
1159—IT HAPPENED ONE WEDDING
1174—MITCH TAKES A WIFE
1188—ALL I WANT FOR CHRISTMAS
1204—THE PILOT'S WOMAN
1252—OOH, BABY!
1266—A FATHER FOR JESSE

Emilio's Chocolate Bourbon Pecan Pie

One unbaked 9-inch pie crust
1/4 cup melted butter
1 cup sugar
3 slightly beaten eggs
3/4 cup light corn syrup
1/4 tsp salt
2 tbsp bourbon
1 tsp vanilla
3/4 cup whole pecans
1 cup semisweet chocolate chips

Sprinkle pecans and chocolate over the bottom of the unbaked pie crust.

Using a mixer, cream together sugar and butter; add eggs, syrup, salt, bourbon and vanilla. Pour over nuts and chocolate. Bake 40-50 minutes. Serve warm or cold with whipped cream.

Eat and die of pleasure…☺

Happy eating!

Chapter One

As Jenny Wyler passed the Saddlers Prairie, One Mile Ahead road sign, she swallowed. The rolling Montana plains were beautiful, with their fields of prairie grass stretching clear to the horizon and plenty of "big sky." The scattered houses and buildings here and there added a nice, welcoming touch.

Great for a getaway.

But living here almost ten months?

Jenny was used to Seattle's snarling rush-hour traffic and bustling activity. Malls, restaurants and coffeehouses galore, movie theaters and fitness centers. None of which was here.

Accepting a teaching job in a one-room school in a place she'd never even heard of until last month was probably a huge mistake.

What in the world had she been thinking?

She signaled. Not that she needed to—her four-door sedan was the only vehicle on the two-lane highway. In the split second before exiting, Jenny considered turning around and backing out of her contract. But school was scheduled to start the Wednesday after Labor Day, a mere five days from now, and she couldn't leave the students without a teacher.

Jenny took the exit. "Buck up, kiddo," she murmured, sounding a lot like her father. "We're Wylers. We adapt."

The paved road stretched in front of her like a dull, gray ribbon. Jenny glanced at the directions Silas and Valerie

Mason had emailed. The Saddlers Prairie Post Office was located in the town center, roughly a mile from here.

With little to distract her, she thought again of her father and all that had happened since his death last October.

If he were still alive, he'd no doubt support this move, especially after what Rob had pulled. Or according to Rob, what *she'd* pulled.

Dad had always counseled her and her older sister, Becca, to keep the past where it belonged—in the past. Desperate to forget, to fit in and be normal like all the other kids, Jenny and Becca had never even mentioned their mother to each other, let alone anyone else.

Which made it all the more ironic that shortly after their father had passed away, the Seattle paper had printed some of the embarrassing details about April Wyler. That she was a schizophrenic who disappeared for weeks at a time and periodically prostituted herself to support a drug habit. When Jenny was seven, her mother had entered a mental institution for counseling and help. Within a few months of moving in, she'd killed herself.

Becca was lucky. She lived in Johannesburg, far away from any fallout from the article. Jenny, on the other hand…

You'd think that in the twenty-first century, the sordid past would barely touch a successful, thirty-year-old teacher. Wrong.

As Jenny drove toward the center of town, memories pelted her like stinging nettles. Coworkers, people she considered friends, had looked at her with surprise, pity and even disgust. Rob's emotions had run deeper and uglier, seesawing between shock and anger. He was her fiancé, and assumed she'd been open and honest with him. About most things, she had.

But she'd hidden the full truth about her mother, and he'd been furious. Also scared, and with good reason. Schizophrenia tended to run in families. Which meant their future children could inherit the mental illness.

Rob didn't want to hear about the medications available to keep the disease in check. Within a few days of learning the truth about Jenny's mother, he'd broken the engagement.

Jenny understood. In his shoes, she'd have done exactly the same thing. At least that's what she told herself.

For one long moment, pain and regret washed over her, and she barely noted the long prairie grass rippling elegantly in the late August wind. Then she squared her shoulders.

With all the upheaval in her life, teaching last year had been rough, to say the least. Compared to that, a year in the boonies, where life was simpler, wouldn't be so bad. No emotional ups and downs, no pretending not to see the appalled expressions on the faces of so-called friends, no wondering who would learn about her mother next. Here, the past was back where it belonged—done with and forgotten.

Jenny *needed* this school year to regroup. While she was here, she intended to fit in and give her best in the classroom. Then, when her contract ended in June, she'd leave.

As if Mother Nature approved of Jenny's craving for normalcy, a sweet, welcoming smell filled the air, reminding her of sun-drenched clover. Only it wasn't clover.

Whatever it was, the lovely smell grew stronger as she neared and passed a neatly lettered sign, Dawson Ranch, Established 1896. A ranch with miles of wood and wire fence that paralleled the road. She saw cows, lots of them, and men on horses. In the distance, the proverbial red barn was visible, along with a white, two-story house with a wraparound porch and other buildings, plus assorted cars, trucks and farm equipment.

After passing the ranch she pulled into the center of town—if that's what you called the gas station, café and weathered shops grouped loosely together around a packed-dirt parking area riddled with potholes.

A lone vehicle was parked near the door of Spenser's General Store, a dusty red pickup. Jenny pulled to a stop a few yards away in front of the post office, a neat, wood building about the size of the one-car garage at the condo she and Rob had shared.

Wanting to make a good first impression, she pulled off her sunglasses, adjusted the visor mirror, then quickly applied lipstick. Thanks to being straight and newly cut just above the shoulders, her hair was easy to smooth. Nothing much she could do about the lap creases in her cotton slacks, though.

She exited the car. After sitting for hours, standing felt good, and she stretched her back.

Just then a lanky male wearing a baseball cap exited the general store, his arms bulging around two giant, burlap bags. Tall and tanned and about her age, he wore faded jeans, a black T-shirt and cowboy boots. Beside him, a little girl with copper-color pigtails who looked about five.

As the big male tossed the bags into the back of the truck, Jenny stared shamelessly, watching his muscles bunch with the effort. He caught her looking. His mouth quirked, and he pulled off his cap, revealing short, dark hair. "Can I help you with something?"

Face warming, she tugged the hem of her cap-sleeve blouse over her hips. "I'm looking for Silas or Valerie Mason."

The man ambled closer, his hand on the little girl's shoulder. "They'll be in the post office."

Which, of course, Jenny knew.

He looked her up and down, his expression unreadable. "You must be the new teacher."

How did he guess? "I am." Jenny extended her hand. "I'm Jenny Wyler."

Though she was five-nine in her summer sandals, this man stood at least half a foot taller. Somber eyes the color of this afternoon's blue Montana sky met her gaze. She noted faint squint lines in the outer corners.

"Adam Dawson." His grip was firm and calloused, and she caught a whiff of grass and man.

"On the way into town, I passed the Dawson Ranch," Jenny said. "Any relation?"

The big man's shoulders straightened with pride. "That's ours—mine and my brother's."

"It looks huge."

"Until two weeks ago, we were sixteen hundred acres and seven hundred Black Angus beef cattle. We just added six hundred acres and two hundred more head."

"I know nothing about ranches and cattle, but that sounds impressive." Jenny smiled.

Adam Dawson did not. In fact, he frowned as if she'd said something wrong. That, or he didn't much like her.

Her cheerful expression wavered before she amped it up again and turned to the little girl, whose eyes were the same deep blue as her father's. "What's your name?"

"This is Abby," her father quickly replied.

She couldn't speak for herself? Ignoring the man, Jenny offered her hand. The girl solemnly shook it, her eyes sparkling, probably because she was excited to be doing something so grown-up.

This time Jenny didn't have to force a smile. "Nice to meet you, Abby. My name is Miss Wyler, and I'm the new teacher at Saddlers Prairie School."

The little girl flashed a matching set of dimples that was utterly irresistible. Charmed, Jenny went on. "You look like you're old enough for kindergarten. Will I see you in class next week?"

For some reason, the question banished Abby's smile. She ducked her head, her attention suddenly riveted on the packed dirt ground.

His frown deepening, her father stepped in front of her. "She'll be there."

He seemed to intimidate his own child. Jenny's protective hackles rose. After shooting him a dirty look, she directed her words at Abby. "That's great. I'll look forward to seeing you on Wednesday."

In the meantime, she'd find out more about Adam Dawson and his wife, whom Jenny hoped wasn't as cowed as her daughter. Jenny certainly wasn't, and gave the imposing man the stern look she reserved for disciplining students.

His eyebrows upped a fraction before he slapped the hat back on his head, dipped his chin, cupped his daughter's shoulder and steered her toward the truck.

Jenny turned away and headed for the post office. By the time she opened the door, Adam Dawson's truck was bumping toward the road.

IN CONTRAST TO THE BRIGHT afternoon sunlight, the post office's fluorescent lighting seemed dark. But the cheerful country-western music song that filled the air made up for the dimness.

A plump, middle-age woman in a sleeveless blouse stood behind a small counter leafing through a magazine, her hair pulled into a loose ponytail. She gave Jenny a cursory look, then reached behind her and turned down the radio. Her apple cheeks rounded in a grin.

"You must be Jenny Wyler," she oozed with warmth and friendliness. The exact opposite of Adam Dawson. "I've been waiting for you. Welcome to town."

"Thank you so much," Jenny said. "I assume you're Mrs. Mason?"

"That always sounds so stuffy. Please call me Val. Silas has the keys to the school and your cottage," she continued, rounding the counter and smoothing a hand over navy summer slacks a size too small. "He's over at Barb's Café, having his afternoon coffee. Come on, and I'll take you over and introduce you."

Jenny barely had a chance to nod before Val hustled her toward the door. "Barb Franklin, who owns the café is also our mayor. She was on that conference call where we interviewed you last month. Her husband, Emilio, and his family settled here from El Salvador a good thirty years ago. At first, the Delgados worked for other people. Now they own a small sheep ranch, run by Emilio's brother. Emilio prefers the restaurant business and always has. He does the cooking and the menus.

"There are several part-time waitresses who come and go, but Donna is always there. She's a real gem. She used to be married, but a good twenty years ago her no-account husband ran off with a gal from Helena, leaving poor Donna with three kids to raise on her own. They're grown now. The boy sells insurance in Missoula. One girl lives with her husband in Boise. The other is divorced and cuts hair on the other side of town. You'll meet her two kids at school."

Val paused to catch her breath, and Jenny marveled at what she'd just learned. Her new acquaintance was a fount of information.

"I noticed you talking to Adam Dawson and little Abby," Val said as they headed across the lot.

She gave Jenny a searching look, and Jenny guessed that her reply would be broadcast far and wide.

"Abby's adorable," she said, skipping over her opinion of the girl's intimidating father.

"She's something, all right."

Val shook her head and clucked her tongue, which only added to Jenny's curiosity. Questions about the man, his child and his wife crowded her mind, questions that Val would no doubt soon answer.

Jenny waited expectantly, but the postal clerk marched ahead.

Pushing through the windowed front door, Val announced to the mostly empty café, "Jenny Wyler is here."

"YOU FINALLY MADE IT," Barb Franklin said as she slid into the booth across from Jenny and Val. "We're awful glad to see you."

Dressed in sneakers, faded jeans and a striped, short-sleeve blouse, she hardly looked like a mayor, let alone a business owner. Emilio, her handsome, graying husband, had flashed a smile from the kitchen, where he was working on something for dinner that smelled heavenly.

"It wasn't until the middle of June that Cheryl Swift told us she was leaving," the mayor went on, shaking her head. "We're lucky that we found an experienced teacher like you, and halfway through the summer."

Jenny sensed the question behind the comment. "Seattle schools cut back, and with the economy still so bad all over the country... I figured that now was a great time to try something different," she said, repeating what she'd said during the phone interview. "I'm looking forward to the challenge of teaching all the elementary grades in one classroom."

Sitting next to Barb, Silas, a balding man in jeans and a button-down shirt that pulled across his belly, stroked his chin with meaty fingers. "What with the harsh weather and the isolation, this ain't no place for sissies. Cheryl Swift only lasted the one year before she hightailed herself back to a big-city school."

Val nodded. "When our kids came up, they had the same teacher from kindergarten to eighth grade," she added wistfully. "Miss Phylinda Graham was a wonderful teacher—strict but also caring. She taught every person at this table, and Donna and Emilio, and we all loved her." Heads nodded. "She taught for forty-five years before she retired some nine years ago. Her replacement stayed two years. Since then, no one has lasted longer than a year."

"Which is a crying shame," Barb said. "Miss Graham lives at Sunset Manor, a retirement home about twenty-five miles northwest of here. She loves to talk about children and learning. If you need advice about teaching in a one-room school, she's your go-to gal."

Jenny mentally stored the information for later use.

"Our children need the stability of a committed teacher who sticks around," Barb continued. "I may as well tell you up front that we all hope that before your contract ends next June, you'll decide to renew."

Jenny wasn't about to divulge her plan to follow in the previous teachers' footsteps and line up a teaching job in an urban area for the following year. Certainly not before she even started working. She added cream and sugar to her mug.

Val snorted. "Don't pressure her, Barb. She's young and real pretty. Why should she be any different than our own sons and daughters? There isn't much to keep a person in Saddlers Prairie."

They were all staring at Jenny now. Offering a weak smile, she tried her coffee. It wasn't Starbucks, but it was freshly brewed and strong, just the way she liked it. "This is really good," she said.

Her stomach promptly growled. She'd last eaten hours ago, a tasteless convenience-store sandwich.

Busy setting the fifteen or so tables and booths for dinner, Donna, who looked to be in her late fifties, chuckled. "I heard that all the way across the room." She bustled over. "Sounds like you need something to go with that coffee. Unfortunately, lunch is over, and we don't start serving dinner for another few hours."

"I know just the thing," Barb said with a grin. "This morning Emilio made a couple of his famous chocolate bourbon pecan pies for the lunch crowd. You're in luck—there's still some left. Dish her up a wedge, Donna."

Jenny licked her lips. "That sounds wonderful."

"Cut me a piece, too," Barb said.

Silas waved his hand. "And me."

"Silas Mason!" Val shot her husband a dirty look. "You know what Dr. Tom said." She glanced at Jenny. "Tom Sackett is the doctor around here. He's a widower and old enough to be your granddad."

"Cody Naylor's closer to your age, sugar," Donna called out. "He just moved back to town. Anita hasn't had any luck with him, but you might."

"Anita is Donna's daughter, the one I told you about, who does hair," Val told Jenny. "Cody's both good-looking *and* single. You'll probably meet him eventually, but if you want, Barb or I could introduce you right away."

The last thing Jenny wanted was anyone fixing her up. Dating could lead to a relationship, which meant the inevitable questions about family. After what had happened with Rob, she wanted none of that. But before she could think of a reply, Barb waved her hand.

"She'll meet him at the Saturday night potluck and dance. That's a few weeks from now, Jenny, in your honor. Our way of welcoming you to Saddlers Prairie."

"That sounds lovely," Jenny said, though she preferred to avoid the limelight.

"It will be," Val answered, frowning at her husband. "Dr.

Tom ordered you to take off thirty pounds. You can bet he'll be eyeing that big belly of yours at the potluck."

"Dr. Tom should talk. He's overweight, too."

When Val pursed her lips, Silas spread his hands out as if to say, *what can a man do?* "I promise I'll cut back, sweet-cakes, but I can't let Barb and the new teacher eat alone, not when they're enjoying one of Emilio's pies. You know you want some, too. How about we share an order?"

Val laughed and shook her head. "All right, I give. But I want my own piece. Did you hear that, Donna?"

Standing behind the counter, the smiling waitress waved the pie cutter. "Already dishing you up some."

Moments later she delivered four generous servings, each topped with homemade whipped cream.

Jenny dug into the slightly warm dessert. The pie melted on her tongue in a delicious blend of chocolate, pecans and a subtle hint of bourbon. She murmured with pleasure. "This is heaven on a plate."

"Did you hear that, Emilio?" Barb hollered.

"I did, and I thank you, Jenny Wyler," the pleased chef replied from the kitchen.

For a moment, everyone was quiet, only the clink of their forks marking the silence.

Soon Val came up for air, trading her fork for her coffee, then wiping her mouth. "Jenny already met Adam and Abby."

For some reason Jenny's face warmed, but none of her tablemates seemed to notice. They were too busy trading glances.

"Abby's a cutie," Jenny said.

"And sweet as this pie." Barb hesitated. "You didn't notice anything about her?"

They all looked at Jenny as if wanting to gauge her next words.

"Well, she seemed a little…" *Intimidated,* but Jenny didn't feel right saying that. "Shy."

"Oh, it's more than that," Barb said. "That little girl doesn't talk."

"Not because she doesn't want to." Val leaned across the table as if confiding a secret. "She can't."

Of all the things Jenny had expected, she'd never imagined this. "You mean she's mute?" she asked.

Silas let out a heavy sigh. "Seems that way."

She glanced at the solemn faces around the table. "Is there a medical reason? Has she been tested?"

"You'd have to ask Adam about that," Barb said. "What isn't about ranching he keeps to himself, so we don't rightly know."

"He didn't used to be so private about his personal doings," Val added, "but the poor man has been to hell and back." Pausing, she took a sip of coffee.

Impatient to hear more, Jenny wanted to tug the cup from the woman's hands and set it down.

Thankfully, Val did that herself. "Not ten days after Abby was born, Simone—that was Adam's wife—died."

Barb let out a heartfelt sigh. "A real tragedy."

No one was eating now, their food forgotten.

"Adam was one of those kids who worked on the ranch a few years before he went off to college at the University of Montana in Missoula," Val continued. "He didn't graduate until he was twenty-five. By then, he was ready for a wife. When he and Simone met at the beginning of senior year, it was love at first sight. A few days after graduation, they got married. Oh, that was a nice wedding."

Everyone murmured their agreement.

"Simone was a professor's daughter," Val went on. "She was supposed to follow in her daddy's footsteps and go on to graduate school, but once she and Adam married, they moved to the ranch to start their lives together."

Barb clasped her hands over her heart. "They were so much in love, you could *feel* it."

Jenny could only imagine what that kind of love felt like. The feelings she and Rob had once shared seemed anemic by comparison.

"Simone got a job teaching English at the high school where the kids from Saddlers Prairie, Deer Creek and a couple other towns go," she continued. "She and Adam had been married all of six months when she got pregnant."

Donna, who wandered over to top off the coffee mugs, joined in the conversation. "Adam was over the moon, remember?"

"Until Simone was about four months along. That's when the doctors found cancer—the kind that grows fast. They wanted to give her chemotherapy, but that was risky to the baby. They suggested abortion so that they could save Simone's life, but she refused. She got sicker and sicker."

Barb took over, her voice a murmur. "Six weeks before Abby's due date, they delivered her by C-section. Ten days later, Simone was gone. Adam was devastated, and then some. A few weeks later, her father had a stroke and died. They say his heart was broken. I know ours were. Now you know."

"How sad," Jenny said, glancing down.

Her opinion of Adam Dawson U-turned. Her heart ached for the man and for the little girl who never had a chance to know her mother, a woman who'd sacrificed her own life for her child.

At least someday Abby would know the depth of her mother's love. For that, Jenny envied the little girl.

"That's enough sorrow for one afternoon." Val set her napkin aside and dismissed the depressing topic. "You're probably eager to get settled in before nightfall. Before you drive off, I suggest you pick up your groceries over at Spenser's and save yourself a trip later."

Silas dug into his hip pocket and held out two keys. "The gold one is to the cottage, and the silver fits the school doors, back and front. Just head west up the road." He pointed out the picture window. "In a few miles you'll see the school. Drive another quarter mile or so to Pinto Road, which is just past the big cottonwood stump on your right. That's your turn. The cottage is about five hundred yards down on your left. Any questions, give a holler."

Chapter Two

Enjoying a rare afternoon coffee break, Adam hooked his boots around the legs of his kitchen chair. "On the way home from town, I stopped by the property we annexed," he said, referring to a small ranch adjacent to theirs, land he and his brother needed for their expanding cattle business. "The crew is making real progress on that barn." He glanced at Drew. "I said you'd be over there this afternoon."

"I was planning to fix that stretch of rusted fence on the north side of the ranch. Can't you go back?"

"Your turn. We both know those men need supervising." They'd hired a few locals for what should've been a repair job, but had turned into a complete rebuild. No one was experienced enough to manage such an extensive construction project.

"Doesn't mean I have to like it," Drew grumbled. "We're spread too thin already, putting in twelve- to fourteen-hour days, with barely a day off here and there. We really need to hire someone to oversee the barn and all the other improvements that need doing over there."

"Tell me about it." As it was, Adam barely had time to eat and sleep. Getting the extra six hundred acres of run-down ranch up and running before winter hit doubled the workload.

Several men had applied for the short-term management

job, but so far they hadn't found anyone with the needed experience.

"Any nibbles from those ads you placed, Megan?" Adam asked Drew's wife.

"Not yet, but we've had a few from the Craigslist posting."

"Great." Adam nodded at Drew. "Do the interviews and let's hire someone."

He was almost finished with his coffee before he spoke again. "When Abby and I picked up the rest of that enriched feed earlier, we met the new teacher."

"You got to meet Jenny Wyler? What's she like?" Megan asked.

"She seems all right." Pretty, too, with big eyes and a full mouth. "She was friendly enough to Abby."

But not to him. Her smile hadn't quite reached her eyes and had quickly turned disapproving.

Adam knew the type better than he knew his own ranch. Big-city woman with no time for a dusty cattle rancher. What she was doing teaching school in Saddlers Prairie was anybody's guess.

"Does she know about…" Drew nodded toward the open back door.

Adam followed his brother's gaze. Abby was sitting under the old poplar that shaded the patch of yard near the barn, cuddling Brianna, the doll Mrs. Ames had given her on her birthday last month.

Stretched out beside his daughter and her doll, Jezebel napped, one black cat paw touching Abby's hip. The two had always been close, maybe because they'd been born on the same sweltering July day. Both had lost their mothers way too early.

Not surprisingly, his little girl spent most of all her time with Jez and the doll. What bothered Adam lately was that every day Abby seemed to withdraw more. Drew, Megan and Mrs. Ames had noticed, too, and they were all worried.

Though for a minute today, his daughter had actually smiled—when the teacher introduced herself. It was a little bright spot that Adam hoped signaled good things to come. Then again...

He shook his head. "Jenny Wyler doesn't know about Abby."

"You gotta tell her," Drew said.

Adam tipped back in the chair, lifting its two front legs off the floor, and crossed his arms. "You might like strangers butting into your life," he muttered, "but I don't."

His younger brother curled his lip. "You don't even like your own family knowing your business." Adam's failure to open up was an old sore spot with Drew.

Megan broke the uncomfortable silence. "You don't have to tell the teacher anything personal, Adam. But for her sake and Abby's, she needs to know about Abby before school starts."

"Guess I don't have much choice." The legs of Adam's chair crashed to the floor.

As much as he wanted to protect Abby, his brother and sister-in-law were right. This was important, even if he didn't expect much to come of talking with the teacher. Why should she be any different from the two experts who'd recently examined his daughter?

He didn't like the pity on his brother and sister-in-law's faces. They'd been married all of three months, and already they thought and acted like a matched pair. But then, they'd been like that since meeting at a rodeo two years earlier.

At least Drew had chosen a woman who enjoyed ranch life and wouldn't threaten to leave. Unlike him.

It was time to get back to work. Adam drained the last of his coffee. "I'd best see to those pregnant heifers."

BRIGHT AND EARLY TUESDAY morning Jenny awoke with one daunting thought. School started *tomorrow*. If that wasn't enough to rattle her nerves, the classroom wasn't quite ready, despite her spending almost the entire three-day weekend working on it.

There was still more to do, and Jenny expected to be over there most of the day.

She wouldn't even think about her six-hundred-square-foot new home, which was almost forty years old and looked every bit of it. At least the place had satellite TV and an internet connection. Not that Jenny had had a second to test either.

Muscles sore from toting supplies, moving and washing desks, and scrubbing the grime off the dirty classroom windows, she stretched gingerly as she padded to the bathroom.

On the way, she glanced past the short hallway to the living room. Unhung pictures and unpacked boxes littered the carpet, and books and folders lay strewn on the slip-covered sofa, the armchair and the knotty pine coffee table.

Just looking at the clutter made her tired, but with so much to do at school, she'd barely taken the time to make her bed, put away the groceries and hang her clothes. The rest would have to wait.

By the time she showered and dressed in jeans and a V-neck shirt, she was eager to tackle the remaining chores in the classroom. Then she'd review the lesson plans for the first day. Eight separate plans, one for each of the eight grade levels of her ten students. Eight grades in the same classroom, at the same time.

The mere thought of that juggling act and the chaos sure to ensue was daunting enough. That Jenny was new to the school and had zero experience teaching in a one-room classroom added a new dimension of anxiety.

She had no appetite for breakfast, but she needed to eat.

While the coffee percolated in a pot that had to be as old as the house, she poured cold cereal into a plastic bowl from the cupboard. After filling a mug of coffee, she brought her breakfast to the scarred oak table that occupied most of the space between the kitchen and living room.

Preoccupied with the day ahead, she shoveled cereal into her mouth without tasting a single bite. Soon after, she washed dishes at the chipped enamel kitchen sink—no dishwasher here. This definitely wasn't the Ritz, but the view was priceless.

Out the open window above the sink, green prairie grass dotted with wildflowers rustled and swayed in the gentle breeze. If she craned her neck to the left, she could see the lone tree in the yard, a tall, leafy thing, shading the bedroom and the back side of the living room. The sweet scent she'd first smelled while driving into town wafted through the window, and largish, mottled-gray birds she'd never seen before wandered through the grass with their chicks.

Jenny was utterly captivated. Too bad there was no one to share this with. A wave of loneliness, unexpected and unwelcome, washed through her. But she was no stranger to being alone, and had chosen to leave Seattle and start fresh in an unfamiliar part of the country where she knew no one.

"People here are nice," she reminded herself. Already Val and Barb had called to check in, and Jenny knew that if she asked, one or both would come running, either for a friendly cup of coffee or to lend a hand with the classroom.

But Jenny wanted to do it all herself. Which was why at the moment she was too busy for a visit, and definitely too busy for a pity party.

She headed purposefully for the living room to grab her purse and leave. As she swung the bag over her shoulder and extracted the keys, footsteps thudded across the front stoop and someone knocked on the door.

Company before eight on a Tuesday morning? Who could it possibly be?

Jenny opened the door and found Adam Dawson there, a large envelope tucked under his arm.

She didn't mask her surprise. "Mr. Dawson. Hello."

"It's Adam."

"Adam. Feel free to call me Jenny—except around the kids."

"Hello, Jenny." Frowning at the doorjamb, he scratched the back of his tanned neck as if standing on her stoop and meeting her gaze made him uncomfortable.

With so much to do today, she wasn't exactly serene and composed herself. But she *was* curious.

Adam glanced at the keys in her hand. "You're about to leave."

"I'm still working on my classroom. What brings you here?"

"I thought you should know some things about Abby before tomorrow—if you can spare a few minutes."

Eager to learn everything she could about the little girl, Jenny widened the door. "I always have time to discuss a student," she said. "Please come in."

As Adam wiped his feet on the wiry doormat and stepped inside, she checked her hair and smoothed her shirt over her hips. He was a big man, and suddenly the little living room seemed even smaller.

Jenny caught a whiff of his clean, spicy aftershave, which seemed at odds with the faded jeans and dark T-shirt. His hair was neatly combed, too. He'd cleaned up for his visit.

Who knew why that made her go all soft inside?

Clutching the envelope, he glanced around at the clutter, his expression impossible to read. Jenny fervently wished she'd put everything away after dinner last night, instead of falling into an exhausted sleep.

"Excuse the mess." Hastily she cleared off the armchair and gestured for him to sit. "I made coffee a little while ago. Would you like some?"

Adam nodded. "Black, please."

She filled two mugs. After handing one to Adam, she made a place for herself on the sofa and sat down.

For a few seconds they sipped in silence, Adam looking everywhere but directly at her. His knees nearly hit the coffee table between them. His broad shoulders were ramrod straight, and the heel of one scuffed-but-clean boot tattooed against the carpet with a rhythmic *thump-thump.*

He was definitely uptight, and apparently wasn't going to start the conversation without a nudge.

Jenny leaned forward. "You wanted to discuss Abby?"

He nodded, then cleared his throat. "My daughter has a problem. She can't talk."

Should she admit that she already knew this? A gut feeling warned her not to. That and Val's comment that Adam Dawson was a very private man. The words slipped out anyway. "I know."

When he gave a questioning look, she explained. "Silas, Val and Barb mentioned it the other day."

Suspicion narrowed his eyes. "What else did they tell you?"

"That your wife died of cancer shortly after Abby was born." Jenny bit her lip. "I'm so sorry, Adam."

His face darkened. "I don't talk about that. It's in the past, where it belongs."

Jenny understood all too well. "I don't talk about my past, either," she said.

By his slightly widened eyes, she knew she'd surprised him. Dreading any questions, she tensed. When none came, she blew out a relieved breath.

Her guest set his cup on the carpet, then pulled a sheaf of papers from the envelope. "I copied these for you."

He reached across the mountain on the coffee table to hand her the papers. His fingers grazed hers, a brief brush of warmth that made her self-conscious and flustered. Jenny's gaze dropped from his broad chest to his flat belly.

She jerked her attention to his face.

Now Adam was staring at her, his eyes dark and hooded. His gaze flicked over her. Something undefined sparked between them, a potent tension that had nothing to do with the past or his daughter.

Unnerved, Jenny scanned the first page of the papers, but her ability to concentrate had all but vanished. She may as well have been trying to read Sanskrit. "What exactly are these?" she asked.

"Reports from a speech therapist and a special-ed expert in Billings."

He'd had Abby tested. For some reason, Jenny hadn't expected that.

Adam Dawson wasn't at all what she'd thought.

WHILE JENNY LEAFED THROUGH the reports that spelled out what the experts called Abby's "learning challenges," Adam studied her. Her top wasn't what you'd call tight, yet the curve of her breasts was hard to miss. He didn't want to notice, so he looked away.

Like him, she apparently had a past she wanted to forget. A part of him itched to find out more. Had she loved someone who despised the very thing that made her happy, the way Simone had hated ranching?

But Jenny's past was none of his business—just as his was off-limits to her.

His wayward gaze lit on her face. Her lips moved while she read. Pursing, straightening, tightening. They pursed again, plump and moist, all but begging him to step over the table and taste. Adam wished they were thin and looked dry and chapped instead, wished she wasn't so pretty.

He sipped his coffee and noted the boxes, books and papers piled everywhere. She sure had a lot of stuff.

She leaned back and crossed her legs. Long legs. Thanks to her jeans, he couldn't see their shape, but he could guess. Images crowded his mind. Her mouth moving under his, her curves soft in his hands. Her thighs cradling his hips...

His body stirred and he shifted in the chair, thanking his maker that Jenny couldn't read his thoughts.

She looked up, caught him staring. Adam snatched his mug off the rug.

Tiny puckers lined the space between her brows. "Would you like more coffee?"

He shook his head, and she went back to reading, though how she could concentrate while she did those gyrations with her mouth...

Adam stifled a groan. His intense reaction to Jenny meant that it was time for a trip to Red Deer, the next town over. It'd been close to a year now since his last visit, a twenty-mile drive out of his way. Time and gas that were necessary expenses, if he wanted his privacy, and Adam did. His only problem was finding the time for the trip.

Sheila, who waitressed at the Buckaroo Tavern in Red Deer, was divorced and always happy to take him into her bed for an hour. Between visits they neither saw nor spoke to each other, an arrangement that worked for them both.

Suddenly Jenny set the papers aside. "I, um, I'm having trouble focusing right now, but I promise I'll read everything carefully before school opens tomorrow. From what I understand so far, Abby seems to have a speech and language delay, as well as trouble processing sounds."

"They say she might never read or speak." Adam snorted.

"And you think they're wrong."

It was a statement, not a question.

"I *know* so. My daughter hears just fine, and she definitely isn't stupid."

"I totally agree," Jenny said, surprising him. "Abby is bright and interested in the world. I could tell by the light in her eyes."

This woman understood what the so-called experts did not, yet she'd only met his daughter for a few short minutes. Despite himself, Adam was impressed.

Hold off, he counseled himself. *You don't know Jenny Wyler at all.*

Yet for the first time in years, he felt hopeful. "She only interacts with my family and the hands who work on the ranch, and doesn't like to be around other kids," he warned. "How do you plan to deal with that?"

"I've never had a student like Abby, and I don't know what I'll end up doing. Give me a few days, and I'll get back to you on that."

Honesty was a rare commodity. Adam's respect for Jenny rose another notch. "Fine."

"Let's set up an appointment to talk again in about a week. How about next Wednesday afternoon?"

"It'll have to be in the evening, after chores. I could stop by around seven-thirty."

She hesitated. "Here at the house again?"

"If it's easier, we could meet at the school."

"Here is fine. By then I should have this mess cleaned up."

"I barely noticed."

"Ha-ha."

Humor lit her eyes, and she smiled, dazzling Adam. A smile of his own slipped out.

Aside from Simone, he'd never seen a prettier woman. Taken aback by feelings he neither liked nor wanted, he set his cup on the pile of books on the coffee table and stood. "I'd best get back to the ranch."

"And I need to get to school." Jenny stood, too. "Wait a minute and I'll walk out with you."

She collected both mugs and deposited them in the kitchen. Seconds later she was back and hooking her purse strap over her shoulder.

Adam moved aside so that she passed through the door ahead of him. Her hips swayed gently. Side by side they sauntered toward her sedan. Despite those long legs, she barely reached his shoulder.

"I'm glad you stopped by, Adam," she said when they reached her car. She tilted her head up, almost as if she wanted his kiss.

That damned mouth again.

He backed away. "Abby and I will see you tomorrow morning."

"Tell her I look forward to that."

He nodded, turned away and made for the truck.

Chapter Three

Wanting to settle Abby at school before the other kids arrived, Adam pulled away from the ranch a good hour early. This was another warm, cloudless summer day, with soaring temperatures predicted. Though in Montana, anytime now the winds could kick up, blowing in the fall weather, with its driving rain and chill temperatures.

He glanced in the rearview mirror at his daughter. "You look real pretty today," he said, silently thanking his new sister-in-law for buying Abby's school clothes. He wouldn't have known what to pick out.

Abby offered a short-lived smile. This morning she couldn't sit still, didn't seem to know what to do with her hands.

"We have time to turn around and get Brianna if you want."

She gave her head a firm shake. She wasn't about to bring a doll to school with her. The squirming and fidgeting continued.

Adam was nervous, too, more than enough for the two of them. Abby didn't have much contact with other kids—her choice—and he worried about their reactions to a mute five-year-old.

He wanted to reach behind him and tug one of her pigtails, but she'd have a fit. Megan and Mrs. Ames had each taken a turn fixing Abby's hair before she was satisfied. "Remember, Miss Wyler knows you can't talk, and she's okay with that," he said to reassure both his daughter and himself.

Her hopeful look made his chest hurt. He wanted so much for her to enjoy school. Liking your teacher helped, and Adam had no doubts about his daughter and Jenny.

She believed Abby was smart, and he'd spent a good deal of time wondering at that. He'd thought a lot about other things, too, that had nothing to do with his daughter.

Jenny's curves, her smooth skin… Was she as soft as she looked?

His body reacted the same way it had in bed last night, hardening painfully. Now it was Adam's turn to shift in his seat. He didn't like this at all. Didn't like thinking about her, period.

Tell that to his brain and his body.

Abby's head was angled, as if she expected him to say something. "You're gonna be fine, I know it," he said, with more conviction than he felt.

That was apparently not what she wanted to hear, for she compressed her mouth in a tight line and turned away to stare out her window.

"Whatcha thinking about, ladybug?"

In the rearview mirror she made a face at him, just as he'd known she would. Hiding a grin, he shrugged. "I know, I know. You're in kindergarten now, and too big for that nickname. It just slipped out."

Her nod and forgiving expression melted his heart. He loved her so damn much.

The road to school was just ahead, and he slowed to turn. Since there wasn't another vehicle in sight, he didn't bother to signal.

"We're just about there." His heart thudded. Because this

was his daughter's first day of school, he told himself. Not because he was about to see Jenny Wyler.

The second Abby caught sight of the white clapboard schoolhouse, her chin jutted up, reminding Adam so much of Simone, he ached. His child shared her mother's stubborn streak, the one that had killed her.

He would never forgive himself for convincing Simone to marry him instead of getting her graduate degree, then talking her into having a child, a desperate measure meant to save their crumbling marriage.

He'd never forgive Simone, either, for refusing treatment for her cancer. But then if she'd taken the chemo, Abby wouldn't be here.

The self-recrimination, anger and anguish that constantly simmered inside him suddenly flared up, and for a few seconds he was lost in darkness.

On automatic pilot he parked in the packed-dirt turnaround, not far from Jenny's car. The front door of the school stood open in welcome, and he came back to himself.

He turned in his seat and glanced at his daughter. "Ready?"

Bravado gone, she swallowed hard. After unbuckling herself from the booster seat, she exited the car. Adam helped her slip into her Mickey Mouse backpack.

As they headed toward the school, she clutched his hand with icy fingers. Outside the threshold, she pulled him to a stop.

There was no sign of Jenny. Adam tasted the sharp tang of disappointment, which he ignored.

Because the door was open, he figured it was okay to go on in. But he didn't rush his daughter, let her look around and tried to see the schoolroom through her eyes.

The place looked the same as it always had—the usual beige walls and weary wood floor, scattered desks of varying sizes facing the teacher's desk. Jenny had tacked colorful posters with alphabet letters and slogans about reading under the school clock, and books and school supplies filled the shelves along one wall. A large whiteboard nearly filled the other, with a similar board up front.

He pointed to the neatly printed words on the whiteboard. "Look at that. She wrote you a message—'Welcome to Miss Wyler's Class.' Let's go in now."

Adam led his daughter forward. The usual smells of paste and old wood permeated the room, taking him back a few years. To a time when his parents and grandparents were still alive, and life was simpler.

"I remember my first day here," he said. "My teacher was Miss Graham, and I had her from kindergarten through eighth grade."

Hadn't taken the woman long to uncover each kid's strengths and weaknesses. Knowledge she'd used to push Adam and his sixteen classmates to work hard, learn and help one another. Drew had been two years behind Adam, and she'd treated him the same way.

He doubted his daughter would be lucky enough to have the same experience. Saddlers Prairie was a low-key place with little appeal, and wouldn't hold an attractive city woman like Jenny Wyler for long.

Suddenly the back door opened. Abby gripped Adam's hand tighter, whether in excitement or fear he didn't know. Clutching a bunch of late-summer prairie wildflowers, Jenny entered the room.

She wore a pale blue dress sprinkled with tiny white hearts, and lace edged her collar and little sleeves. Adam liked the dress, liked seeing her slender legs, which were every bit as shapely as they were in his fantasies.

"Oh!" she said, looking surprised. "I didn't know anyone was here yet."

His face warmed. "Thought I'd get Abby settled in before the other kids arrive."

"That's a great idea."

Jenny met his gaze with her big, expressive eyes. Green, he noticed for the first time, and very bright.

She turned her attention to his daughter. "Good morning, Abby. What a pretty yellow dress! Go ahead and put your backpack in the cubby over here. Yours is the one that says, *Abby.* Can you find it?"

Abby stared at the brightly painted wooden shelves for a moment. Her shoulders slumped, and she shook her head.

"No problem, I'll help you. This one is yours. *A-B-B-Y* spells *Abby.* This year you'll learn to read and write your name, as well as to add and subtract and all sorts of other wonderful things. Sound fun? Now please put your backpack away."

When Abby did as she was told, Jenny smiled. "Good job. Now, how about helping me with these flowers? I think this empty mayonnaise jar will make a nice vase."

Adam's little girl nodded and joined Jenny at the teacher's desk.

He stood back, watching the woman show his daughter how to fix the flowers so that they looked pretty in the jar. Jenny treated Abby like any other kid, and Abby responded with rare enthusiasm. Any stranger who happened in would think she was normal.

Gratitude filled Adam—among other warm feelings he wasn't about to examine.

Now that he knew Abby was fine, he could leave. Ought to. Plenty of chores waited on the ranch. Fence to mend, cattle to vaccinate, alfalfa and hay to bale.

The crew that worked on the ranch could handle the bulk of it, but the more hands, the better. Plus Adam needed to be there for the unexpected emergencies that always sprang up, especially with Drew being busy both supervising the barn construction on their annexed property and interviewing a potential construction manager.

Yet Adam didn't move. Couldn't take his eyes off Jenny. He liked watching her with Abby, her expression soft and kind, respectful. Nurturing.

She was beyond pretty. She was beautiful.

Hardly aware of what he was doing, he gawked like a man bewitched. Jenny and Abby finished with the flowers and still he stared.

"See what Abby and I just did," Jenny said. "She's a terrific helper."

His daughter beamed, something she rarely did.

Jenny's smile was brighter than a ray of sunshine. Packing a wallop that went straight to Adam's chest. And to his groin. He swallowed, but didn't lower his gaze.

Recognition flashed in her eyes, as if she, too, felt something. A fine tension, the kind that only happened between a man and a woman, simmered the air.

Her smile faltered, and she turned away to fuss with one of the flowers. "I know how busy you are, Adam. Don't worry about Abby—we'll be just fine. Unless...was there something you wanted?"

Oh, yeah, but those things were better left unsaid. He cleared his throat, then like a fool struck dumb, said nothing.

"Abby, I'm going to talk to your daddy for a few minutes outside," Jenny said. "While I'm gone, why don't you try out your desk? It's all ready for you. See, there's your name card, right on top." She pointed out one of the smaller desks at the front of the room.

Abby nodded eagerly. When Adam moved to kiss her goodbye, she shook her head.

First leaving Brianna home, now shunning a kiss from her dad... She was growing up way too fast.

"Megan will pick you up, ladybu—Abby," he reminded her. He glanced at Jenny. "That's Abby's aunt."

His daughter signaled that she understood. She was sitting at the desk, swinging her legs, when Adam followed Jenny through the front door.

As JENNY WALKED AHEAD of Adam, she swore she felt his gaze on her rear end. Adam Dawson unsettled her, and wasn't she already nervous enough this morning? Self-conscious, she hurried along.

The second they both cleared the door, she spun toward him. Ears reddening, he snatched his attention to her face. He *had* been checking her out.

How long had it been since a man had found her attractive? It seemed like ages, and she had to admit his interest more than flattered her. He was pretty great to look at himself. Plus she was genuinely starting to like this man.

Regardless, she wasn't about to encourage him in any way. She wouldn't be in Saddlers Prairie that long, and besides, involvement meant the inevitable questions about her family. Questions she preferred to leave buried, because although lies didn't work so well, the truth was even worse.

Squinting against the already bright day, she looked up at him. He moved a little so that his body blocked out the sun.

"What's on your mind, Adam?" she asked, appreciating his thoughtfulness.

"Just…" He shifted and kicked at the packed dirt at his feet. "I wanted to thank you for treating Abby like that."

"Like what?"

"A regular kid."

Suddenly it all made sense—the intense looks, the warmth burnishing his eyes. What Jenny had mistaken for sexual attraction was nothing more than simple gratitude.

If that didn't prove how starved she was for a man's attention… *Pathetic, Jenny, just pathetic.*

Also unbelievable. Here she was having heart palpitations over the father of what could be her most challenging student ever, a man she didn't want to get involved with in the first place. Jeez Louise.

Grateful that the man facing her had no clue what she was thinking, she pushed her wayward thoughts aside. "Abby's a sweet little girl," she said, smiling her let-me-reassure-you teacher smile.

Adam didn't look one bit reassured. He certainly wasn't smiling. In fact, the corners of his mouth turned down.

"You're worried about her," Jenny guessed, her heart breaking for the man and his motherless child.

"Like I told you yesterday, she hasn't had much contact with other kids. She prefers to keep to herself."

It sounded as though she took after her father, if what Val, Silas and Barb said was true. "After I accepted this job, I did lots of research on one-room schools," Jenny said. "I have some terrific ideas for keeping the children engaged with one another." Behind her back, she crossed her fingers.

"What if Abby won't interact with the other kids? What if they don't want to be around her, either? I don't expect they'll think much of a girl who's different."

Having spent her own first seven years enduring the stigma of living with a schizophrenic mother, Jenny knew all too well how that felt. She wasn't about to sit back the way her teachers had, and let Abby or any other child suffer needlessly. "I won't tolerate cruelty of any kind. That I promise you."

Adam still looked unconvinced, so she touched his forearm in a gesture of understanding and comfort. She felt warmth and taut strength. An instant later he jerked away as if she'd burned him or worse.

Apparently she'd overstepped. Schooling her expression as she'd learned to do when she was four, the first time the police had delivered her disheveled mother home and the neighbors had gaped and whispered, Jenny pretended that nothing had happened, and all was well. "I'll watch over Abby. I know she'll be fine."

"Fine? She *can't talk.*"

His refusal to even glimpse the possibilities, to trust that Jenny would smooth Abby's way, irked her. "Why are you so angry with *me,* Adam? I'm trying to help!"

His jaw snapped shut in surprise. He scrubbed the back of his neck, which he seemed do to a lot of. "I—"

A black Jeep rumbled into the parking area, cutting him off. A dozen yards behind, a minivan and an SUV followed.

Embarrassed by her outburst, Jenny apologized. "I'm sorry I raised my voice."

"Forget it, it was my fault." His eyes flashed remorse before he nodded at the vehicles. "The minivan belongs to Jess and Connie Volles. He's in the forest service, and she works part-time at Spenser's. Louisa Bennett is Sheriff Gabe Bennett's wife, and she drives the Jeep. The SUV belongs to Anita Eden. She does hair."

The second the engines shut off, five children—half the class—spilled out, and there was no time for apologies or anything else.

All three women were about Jenny's age, and as friendly as everyone else she'd met. Right away she liked them and their kids. She greeted bouncy, blonde Suzanne Volles, a second-grader, and her sturdy-looking, fifth-grade brother, Martin. She welcomed dark haired, energetic Charlie Bennett, who was also starting second grade, Julie Eden, a gangly seventh-grader, and Edgar, her younger brother, a fourth-grader.

Next time Jenny glanced around, Adam was gone.

WHEN MRS. AMES RANG THE lunch bell after several back-breaking hours spent baling the last of the wild hay and alfalfa, everyone but Adam and the foreman, Colin, turned as one and strode toward the two Jeeps, part of the small fleet the crew used to get around the ranch when they weren't riding the horses.

"You coming?" Colin asked.

Adam's stomach was empty, and he'd been on his feet for hours. He needed to sit down and eat. He also needed a moment of solitude. "In a minute."

"We'll leave you one of the Jeeps, then."

Adam pulled off his baseball cap and swiped his forehead with his arm. He eyed the bales with satisfaction. They were about half-done, right on schedule.

Other hands were mending fence, or riding herd, moving cattle toward what remained of the alfalfa pasture after the harvest, and picking up strays along the way.

Drawing in a breath of alfalfa- and hay-sweetened air, he took in the rolling ranch land that seemed to stretch on forever. He enjoyed working hard, pushing himself physically. Usually the combination of sore muscles and quiet cleared his head and filled him with satisfaction.

Not today. Thoughts buzzed around his mind like pesky gnats. Was Abby doing all right? Did she like school, and was Jenny looking out for her?

Adam figured she was. Even if she was annoyed with him. His fault, but he'd needed to push her away. Because when she'd touched him…

Here it was, hours later, and he still felt the gentle warmth of her fingers on his forearm. He hadn't felt that kind of connection in a while, and he'd almost lost it, had almost pulled her close and kissed the bejeezus out of her, right there in front of the school.

A certain part of him started to rise. Gritting his teeth, he slapped his hat back on his head and stalked to the Jeep. He didn't see the mole hole before he stumbled and twisted his ankle.

It hurt like a son of a bitch, and he let out a string of obscenities. He hoped he hadn't sprained it. On the positive side, the pain took care of any lingering-touch nonsense.

Yet he still felt twitchy and hot.

Well, hell.

With that, he made up his mind. He'd drive to Red Deer and see Sheila tonight, satisfy the craving that had him wanting a woman he had no business wanting.

That ought to work.

Chapter Four

By the time Jenny hustled her class outside for midmorning recess, she was beyond ready for a break. Standing under the eaves shading the back of the school, she watched her students play without really seeing them.

She was too distracted by the realization that she was in way over her head.

Her seven years as a teacher definitely helped, as did her extensive research on teaching in a one-room school. Knowing that she needed to prepare for every grade from kindergarten through grade eight, she'd spent countless hours on lesson plans. She'd also planned half a dozen activities to kick off the school year, and had come to work rested and ready for a great first day.

Yet for all her experience and preparation, she'd realized within the first hour how woefully unprepared she really was. Juggling the needs of the ten students of different ages and grades wasn't easy.

Abby presented the biggest challenge. Once the other children had begun to arrive this morning, the excitement and eagerness the little girl had displayed earlier had vanished. Abby had tucked her chin to her chest and retreated to a place Jenny couldn't seem to reach.

No amount of smiling or encouragement helped. The little

girl simply refused to respond. Small wonder the two experts who'd tested her had come up with dire results.

But Jenny knew better. If she could just coax Abby out of her shell and help her gain confidence…

The big question was, how?

We're only a few hours into the first day of school, she reminded herself. She would contact Phylinda Graham soon, possibly later today, and ask for insight and advice.

Jenny glanced at her only kindergartner, who lingered near her, watching the other children with a longing expression that reminded Jenny of herself as a child. Her throat tightened in sympathy.

Oblivious, the other nine students raced around, calling out and laughing in the warm sunshine, using up some of the boundless energy they all seemed to possess. Even the two oldest, eighth-grader Jonas Borden and seventh-grader Julie Eden joined in, chasing the younger kids between the swings, under the basketball hoop and across the grassy field.

Doing her best to seem nonchalant, Jenny wandered toward Abby. "Wouldn't you like to play with the other children? I'm sure they'd love for you to join in."

The girl ducked her head and shook it furiously.

When three giggling girls skipped toward the swings, Jenny called out to them. "Emily, Suzanne and Olivia, will you please come over here?"

The six-, seven- and eight-year-old girls trotted over.

"I'd like you to include Abby in your game," Jenny said.

A look of terror crept over Abby's face, but none of the other three seemed to notice.

"Do you know how to jump rope?" Suzanne asked.

Abby stared at the ground, while Emily, who was in first grade, clapped her hands. "I do, and I love to jump!" Her grin exposed gaps where she'd lost her front teeth. "It's really fun, Abby."

"We don't care if you can't talk," Olivia, the third-grader, added. "As long as you take your turn twirling the rope while one of us jumps. Do you know how?"

"When I was five, I didn't," Emily replied with a now-that-I'm-six-I'm-big-and-wise tone that had Jenny smiling.

"I'll show you how to move the rope and how to jump," Jenny offered. She took Abby's hand and gently tugged.

The little girl's gaze remained fixed on the ground and she dragged her feet, but she allowed Jenny to pull her forward. Despite Abby's refusal to participate, Jenny noticed that she watched the girls out of the corner of her eye. Once or twice her little lips almost curled into a smile.

It was a start.

OFF TO PICK UP ABBY, Megan honked as her white SUV trundled down the quarter-mile driveway.

Adam paused to wave. Ankle throbbing, he'd left the rest of the baling to the crew and turned instead to equally hard work that demanded less of his ankle—mending fence. He was working with a seasoned hand named Lou, while his horse, Flicker, grazed nearby.

"She going to pick up Abby?" Lou asked, whipping off his baseball cap to swipe his brow.

Adam nodded. Eager to greet his daughter and find out about her day, he added, "When they come back, I'll take a break. You deserve one, too."

"I'd rather keep on so that we finish this stretch before dark," Lou said. "But leave me the thermos and I'll sip a cup of that coffee."

"That'd be good."

There the conversation, such as it was, ended. Lou wasn't a big talker, which suited Adam fine. They continued working in tandem, Lou digging out a rusted post, and Adam shoving in its replacement, making sure the new post stood straight, then anchoring it in the ground. Then Adam secured a new length of barbwire to the post while Lou dug out another.

The kind of work that required focus and muscle. Even so, waiting for Abby wasn't easy. Time seemed to drag, Adam's thoughts straying like a lost calf searching for its mama.

What was taking so long? The school was only a ten-minute drive away. Was Jenny giving Megan an earful about Abby? About *him?* Adam sure hoped not.

The wondering was almost worse than the waiting.

A good thirty minutes later, the SUV at last rolled up the driveway.

Adam pulled off his scarred leather work gloves. "I'll be back."

He tossed Lou the thermos, mounted Flicker with barely a wince, and raced across the field.

By the time Adam dismounted and tethered Flicker near the barn, Megan was opening the back door of her car to let Abby out.

A whir of black, Jez streaked across the lawn to greet her, more like a dog than a cat.

Abby exited the car with a pinched face and a death hold on her doll. Adam's hopes that she'd enjoyed her first day of school plummeted.

"I brought Brianna along in case," Megan explained in a low voice. "And a good thing I did."

"So I see." In a louder voice, Adam called out, "Hey, Abby."

His daughter glanced at him and nodded before dropping to her knees to hug Jez, without letting go of Brianna. By the cat's loud purr, she didn't mind.

Seconds later they headed for the house, Jez trotting after them.

Adam favored his right leg, earning a questioning look

from both his daughter and his sister-in-law. "I twisted my ankle in the north pasture this morning," he said. "Nothing to worry about." He cupped his daughter's narrow little shoulder. "I'm more interested in hearing about you, Abby. How was your first day of school?"

Her stricken look made him wish he hadn't asked.

"I think it went well," Megan said brightly. "Jenny—Miss Wyler—seems very nice, and the kids are friendly, too." Over Abby's head she gave a confirming nod.

Good to know, but what mattered was Abby. And she definitely wasn't happy.

Megan stopped at the barn. "I'd best get back to sorting the horse tack." She handed over Abby's backpack. "There's a letter in there about homework, what to expect and stuff like that." Leaning down, she gently tugged one of Abby's now-lopsided pigtails. "I'll see you at dinner tonight."

Even before they reached the house, Mrs. Ames had the screen door open and a welcoming smile on her face. "Hey there, Miss Kindergarten. I'll bet you're hungry after your big day."

Abby hung her head, and the housekeeper's smile slipped. She glanced at Adam, and he shook his head.

"It just so happens, I baked a batch of your favorite cookies this morning—snickerdoodles," Mrs. Ames went on. "The crew ate most of them at lunch, but we saved you some."

She gestured at the cookie jar. "Go on and change your clothes, then wash up. I'll fix you up with a couple of extra-big cookies and a nice glass of milk."

An offer like this didn't come every day. When it did, Abby usually lit up.

Today she gave a lackluster nod that squeezed Adam's heart. He squinted hard at her. She *was* a shade or two paler than normal. Maybe she was coming down with something.

"Come here and let me feel your forehead," he said. No fever. He frowned. "What's bothering you, ladybug?"

Despite his use of the "baby" nickname, he didn't get so much as a scolding look.

Mrs. Ames tsked. "You're worn out after your first day of school, aren't you, kiddo? I know you're a big girl and you've given up naps, but you could probably use one this afternoon."

Abby didn't argue. She scooped up Jez and regarded Adam with the big-eyed, pleading look he'd never been able to resist.

"All right," he said, grudging but accepting. "Jez can sleep with you, but just this once."

"I'm almost through putting dinner together," Mrs. Ames said. "I don't mind helping Abby change and tucking her in. That way you can get back to work."

Adam nodded. "Don't let her sleep more than half an hour, or she'll never settle down tonight."

With his daughter so down in the dumps, he changed his mind about driving to Red Deer to see Sheila tonight. His physical needs would have to wait.

He needed to ride back to the north pasture and help Lou finish that stretch of fence. He also needed to find out more from Megan. As he entered the big barn, the scent of horses and hay met him like old friends. Afternoon light slanted through the windows and open door, creating sharp shadows across the neatly swept floor.

Megan was at the back of the lofty building, sorting tack into piles. "Some of this stuff is beyond repair," she said.

"Order what you need. Abby's taking a nap. She also turned down Mrs. Ames's snickerdoodles." He gave his head an incredulous shake. "Was she this low when you picked her up?"

"She was, but that's nothing to worry about. Six hours, a big chunk of them spent sitting at a desk, makes for a long day. Especially for a five year old. Abby's exhausted, but kids adapt pretty easily. She'll get used to the routine in no time."

Adam hoped his sister-in-law was right. "This is Abby we're talking about. She isn't good with change."

"I know, Adam, but she has to go to school. Let's give her a chance."

Unless he wanted to go the homeschool route, and he didn't, he didn't have much choice. "Did Jenny say anything about how Abby did?" he asked.

"She couldn't—not in front of Abby or the other kids and their parents. I really like Jenny, Adam. Besides being friendly, she seems nurturing and tuned into her students—exactly the kind of teacher Abby needs. And I found out that, like me, Jenny's a big reader. She'd make a super addition to the book club, and I'm going to check with Louisa and Carol about asking her to join. Before I forget," Megan dug into her jeans pocket and pulled out a slip of paper, which she gave to Adam. "Jenny said she forgot to give you her phone number this morning. She handed it out to all the parents and said to call anytime. I'm sure she'll happily answer your questions over the phone."

Because Adam wanted to call her, and not just to discuss his daughter, he shook his head. "We set up a meeting for next week. I'll find out how Abby's doing then. If something goes really wrong before then, I'm sure Jenny will get ahold of me."

Already he looked forward to that meeting, to seeing Jenny Wyler. Just the two of them. Alone.

Get your mind out of that gutter.

Momentarily forgetting his twisted ankle, Adam turned for the barn door. Damned thing hurt like hell, just penance for his wayward thoughts. He winced.

Megan bit her lip. "You sure that ankle's okay?"

"I'll live."

Chapter Five

At last, Friday afternoon arrived and school ended. With a sense of relief Jenny locked the school doors and headed for her car. She'd survived the first week.

Make that blundered through. She'd made enough mistakes to last the whole school year. Nothing had quite gone as planned, but then, did it ever?

"I'll do better next week," she told the poplar opposite the parking area. "Once I've caught up on my sleep."

Much as she wanted to go home, crawl into bed and stay there until morning, she couldn't. She'd scheduled a four-thirty meeting with Phylinda Graham.

Turning her car in the opposite direction from the cottage, Jenny followed the highway toward Sunset Manor, the retirement home where Miss Graham lived.

In most cities, four o'clock signaled the start of rush hour. In Saddlers Prairie, the highway was as deserted as when Jenny had first pulled into town exactly one week ago. Light traffic seemed pretty much a constant.

The rolling prairies were a different story. Overnight, the grass had begun to change color, the rich emerald-green paling. The prairie flowers, too, looked droopier and faded. Jenny still smelled the sweet scent she now identified as alfalfa, but late in the day, the wind felt sharper. Autumn was definitely nudging summer aside.

Thanks to an interesting radio talk show about cattle—Jenny learned that this was the time of year to wean calves from their mothers and to pregnancy-test cows—in what seemed no time, she spotted the black-and-white Sunset Manor sign. She pulled into the paved parking lot of a surprisingly modern-looking brick building.

Moments later she stepped through the automatic door and into a brightly lit lobby filled with comfortable-looking furniture and vases of fresh flowers. She stopped at the reception desk near the door, where a slender, regal-looking woman in a coral pantsuit, her hair in a neat silver bun greeted her. Behind her bifocals, warm brown eyes added a friendly welcome.

"Hi," Jenny said. "I'm Jenny Wyler, and I'm here to see Miss Graham."

"I thought you might be she." The older woman's smile widened, causing the crease lines around her eyes to deepen. "I'm Miss Graham."

Her handshake was firm yet feminine, and her gaze, direct and assessing.

"I had no idea you *worked* here," Jenny said.

"I don't." The older woman lowered her voice. "The receptionist needed to visit the ladies' room, so I offered to fill in."

Her eyes seemed to twinkle, and Jenny liked her all the more.

The receptionist, a woman who wasn't much younger than Miss Graham, returned.

"If you don't mind, we'll sit in the library," Miss Graham said. "At this hour it should be empty. It's this way, just off the lobby."

All of five feet two inches tall, she strode forward at a fast clip, leading Jenny to a modest room filled with shelves of paperback books. They sat down across from each other at a small table.

Miss Graham folded her hands on the table and inclined slightly forward, and Jenny pictured her sitting behind a teacher's desk the same way.

"Tell me about your classroom," she said, her brown eyes bright and interested.

Jenny talked briefly about her students, and what she wanted to do. "Teaching in a one-room school is a lot harder than I expected," she finished.

"Don't I know it. If you said it was easy, I wouldn't believe you."

"I've made so many mistakes. I've noticed that while I work with some of the needier students, the rest seem bored and unhappy. They act out and I get frustrated with them, which doesn't help them or me."

"Children are amazingly understanding and forgiving, especially if they know you care."

"I care. A lot." To Jenny's shock, her eyes filled with tears, which she hastily swiped away. "I guess I'm feeling a little overwhelmed."

"When I first started, I did, too. Keep an open mind and be flexible, and you'll get it right."

"That's good advice," Jenny said. "If you have any tips, I'd love to hear them."

Miss Graham gave Jenny so many suggestions, she pulled out a notebook and began scribbling notes. From time to time, she posed questions.

The older woman nodded approvingly. "I sense that you have the makings of a terrific one-room schoolteacher."

"Really? Thank you." The praise seemed genuine and meant a lot. Jenny felt as if she'd been awarded a gold medal. If this was how Miss Graham praised her students, it was no wonder they'd adored her.

"There is one particularly difficult situation with my kindergartner," Jenny added. "I believe you had her father in class—Adam Dawson?"

Miss Graham lit up. "I remember Adam. A nice young man, and smart as a whip. He and Drew come from good stock, and I should know. As a young teacher, I taught their parents. Adam could be quite mischievous. I recall the time he stole all my chalk—at that time the school still used chalkboards. As I had nothing to write with, Adam suggested I dismiss school for the day. The suggestion and his too-innocent expression prompted me to question him. Eventually he produced the chalk from his desk."

Jenny couldn't even imagine serious Adam ever pulling a stunt like that. She smiled. "What did you do?"

"Made him clean the blackboards for the next month." Miss Graham laughed. "He took his punishment like a man, and did an admirable job. My blackboards looked like new." After a moment, she sobered. "I haven't seen him since his wife's funeral. Cradling his infant daughter in his arms, too numb and grief-stricken to cry. You don't forget something like that. How is he?"

Once again Jenny's heart ached for the man who'd endured so much sorrow. "Fine, I guess. I don't see much of him."

She hadn't spoken with him since he'd dropped off Abby at school on Wednesday morning, but she'd certainly thought about him. The way he looked at her. Flinching when she touched his arm as if she was being too familiar.

Then the sudden realization that he wasn't attracted to her at all, only grateful to her for being kind to his daughter.

That was a big relief really. All the same, scalding heat rushed to her cheeks.

Hoping Miss Graham didn't notice, Jenny managed a neutral shrug. "He's busy with his ranch, and his sister-in-law, Megan, drops Abby off and picks her up." The woman's shrewd look told Jenny she *had* noticed. "Megan has invited me to join her book club," she rushed on. "The two other members are mothers of my students, and we're meeting to-morrow afternoon."

"How lovely that you're making friends so quickly," Miss Graham commented. "You were telling me about Abby Dawson."

"Right. Abby doesn't speak and never has."

"So I've heard." Miss Graham gave her head a sympathetic shake. "How is she coping with school?"

Not sure how much to divulge without Adam's permission, Jenny summarized, "We just finished our first week, which was only three days, so I can't really say yet. I do know that I've never dealt with such a challenging situation."

"Tell me about what's going on, from the beginning."

With that simple request, Jenny poured out the whole story. Starting with the sweet, little girl who showed up every morning in a pretty dress and neatly fixed hair. "She usually arrives before the other children," she said. "That's when she seems the most open and excited about the day ahead, and then *I* get hopeful that the new day will be better than the one before."

Hopes left unfulfilled. Jenny explained how lessons, recess and even lunch consisted of her struggles to engage Abby. She listed the various ways she'd attempted—and failed—to encourage the girl to participate and feel welcome. Experiences that proved difficult not only for Abby and Jenny, but for the rest of the children, as well, who bore witness to the daily frustrations.

Last, she shared the results of the tests from the two experts Adam had hired. "I think they're wrong—Abby is a smart little girl with loads of potential," she finished. "I just don't know how to get through to her."

Miss Graham nodded. "How do the other children respond to her?"

"They're a friendly group. Someone is always offering to play with her or include her in activities, both in the classroom and on the playground. She watches them out of the corners of her eyes, and I know she wants to join in, but unfortunately no matter what the students or I do or say, she won't participate."

"Mmm-hmm." Miss Graham tapped a finger bent with arthritis thoughtfully over her lips. "I happen to know of someone, the daughter of a longtime friend, who may be able to help. She's a speech—"

Whatever she was about to say was interrupted by a group of elderly seniors shuffling past the library, waving and calling out hellos.

"Coming to dinner, Phylinda?" a dapper-looking octogenarian asked.

"Hello, Henry. Is it that time already?" Miss Graham checked her watch. "Goodness, Jenny, we talked right up to mealtime. The food here is surprisingly good. I hope this doesn't offend you, but I wasn't comfortable inviting you to dinner without meeting you first. Now that I have, I'd like to get to know you better and talk more about your classroom and Abby Dawson. Will you join me for dinner?"

After a week of solitary evening meals, mostly consisting of sandwiches or scrambled eggs, Jenny couldn't pass up the invitation. She smiled at her mentor and new friend. "I'd love to."

TO JENNY'S PLEASED SURPRISE, she received an email from her sister Saturday morning. Busy tracking a troop of monkeys, Becca had been out of touch for over a month. She wanted to know about Saddlers Prairie, and also wanted to Skype soon. Jenny sent back a time, along with a newsy post about her school and the town.

Becca's email and anticipation of this afternoon's book-club meeting put Jenny in high spirits. Humming, she filled the rest of the morning with household chores and reviewing the book selection, which she'd read months earlier.

The club members took turns hosting the get-togethers in their homes, with this month's meeting at Louisa Bennett's house. After lunch, with driving directions and book in hand, Jenny pulled onto the highway. Today was another warm, sunny day, and the air smelled particularly sweet.

She parked in front of the neat, ranch-style house. Carol Borden, whose son, Jonas, was the eighth grader in Jenny's school, was just exiting her car. Jenny greeted the woman with a smile. "Hi, Carol."

Carol, too, smiled. "Hey, there, Jenny. You look rested today."

"I am, thanks to a good night's sleep."

In addition to a copy of the book, Carol clutched a Tupper-ware container. Jenny bit her lip. "Was I supposed to bring something?"

Carol shook her head. "Just yourself this first time, but after today, you'll want to bring a snack." She knocked on the door, then, without waiting for someone to answer, opened it and poked her head inside. "I'm here and so is Jenny," she called out.

"Come on in." Louisa's voice came from the back of the house. "Megan and I are making coffee."

Jenny followed Carol into Louisa's country-themed kitchen.

"Welcome to my home, Jenny," Louisa said.

Like Carol, she was about Jenny's age, a tiny woman with short dark hair and large gray eyes. Jenny greeted Megan, who was loading a tray with cookies and brownies that smelled delicious.

"What can I do to help?" she asked.

"We need milk for the coffee," Louisa replied. "There's a pitcher in the fridge, if you want to get it. Put it beside the sugar bowl."

While Jenny complied, Carol opened her Tupperware container and added lemon bars to the tray.

"It all looks so good," Jenny said, wishing she'd eaten a smaller lunch.

"And tastes even better." Meg's eyes sparkled. "But don't worry, there are no calories in anything eaten during book club."

Jenny laughed. "Where's Charlie? I'd like to say hello." The boy was one of her two second graders.

"He's at a friend's house this afternoon, and was sorry he didn't get to see you. Gabe's working today." Louisa winked. "Our husbands and kids know to make themselves scarce during our meetings."

The women exchanged nods. Having neither husband nor child, Jenny would've easily felt left out if they hadn't included her in their knowing grins.

"I'll let Charlie know you asked about him." Louisa waved her hand toward the cups and saucers, then hefted the tray. "Help yourself to coffee, everyone, then follow me into the living room."

Ten minutes later, seated in a cozy armchair with her coffee and a plate of goodies within reach on the coffee table, Jenny felt comfortable and relaxed.

"I'm curious," Carol said. "How does teaching here compare with teaching in Seattle?"

Jenny wasn't going to lie. "Teaching eight grades in one room is a new challenge for me, but I'll get the hang of it."

"I've heard that Seattle is a great place to live," Megan

said. "It's so cool that you moved to little Saddlers Prairie.
You said you wanted to try something different, but choos-
ing to live here seems like a *huge* change."

All three women eyed Jenny curiously, and she knew they
expected an explanation. "My fiancé and I split up," she said,
"and I wanted to start fresh."

They made sympathetic sounds and looked eager to know
more. Wanting to stave off their questions, Jenny hurried on.
"I met with Miss Graham yesterday, and she gave me some
excellent tips on teaching in a one-room school."

About to reach for a brownie, Louisa paused. "That's right,
you drove over to Sunset Manor after school. What do you
think of her?"

"She's wonderful, and still so enthusiastic about teaching,"
Jenny said.

"That doesn't surprise me one bit. Miss Graham was my
teacher for eight years, and I adored her. Everyone in school
did. Drew and Adam, and my own Gabe, attended right along
with me. She expected a lot, and worked us hard, but we
knew she truly cared about us."

Wanting to convey the same things to her own students,
Jenny nodded and reached for her mug.

"Speaking of my brother-in-law," Megan said. "What do
you think of him, Jenny?"

Not sure what she was asking, Jenny took a long sip of
coffee and thought about how to reply. "He seems like a
caring father," she finally said.

To Jenny's relief, the conversation turned to other things.
Food, local gossip and TV shows, all punctuated with laughter. In no time, a lively discussion started, interspersed with
more laughter, coffee and snacking.

Two hours later, Carol glanced at her watch. "I have to
scoot. I promised Jonas I'd drive him to his cousin's sleepover

birthday party in Glendive. What book shall we read for next month's meeting?"

Jenny left the Bennett home with the name of a new book to read and three new friends. Living in Saddlers Prairie wasn't going to be half bad.

AFTER SCHOOL ON WEDNESDAY afternoon, Jenny drove home with no idea of how she got there. She was too distracted about her appointment with Adam tonight.

"He's Abby's father, nothing more," she repeated in the car—as she had throughout the day.

She imagined the evening's conversation, she and Adam sitting across the coffee table, discussing his daughter. Teacher to parent, Jenny friendly and concerned, and focused solely on Abby's welfare. As she should.

No amount of logic or reason slowed the anticipation humming through her. After a dinner she barely tasted, she fluffed the colorful throws she'd bought at Spenser's, and ran the vacuum over the already spotless carpet. Then she freshened up, taking extra care with her makeup and hair.

Why was she doing this? Aside from being Abby's teacher, Adam didn't care about her or her home. And a good thing, too, since she'd be gone in less than a year. Even if he were interested, and he wasn't, she certainly didn't want to start anything with him. Another point she reminded herself several times.

Jenny was in the kitchen when she heard his truck rumble to a stop in the driveway. Moments later, he knocked at the door.

Her stomach fluttered. She checked her hair, caught herself and frowned. Tonight was about Abby, period. "Concerned and friendly, but distant," she repeated the instant before she opened the door.

She pasted a smile on her face. The wind gusted, blasting air with a distinct chill into the house and right through Jenny's hair. So much for smooth and neat.

She chafed her arms. "It's windy tonight! Hello, Adam. Please come in."

Adam wiped his feet and stepped across the threshold. "This breeze is mild compared to what comes later."

By his damp hair and freshly shaved face, he'd just showered. He smelled as good as he had the last time he was here.

He was dressed in the usual T-shirt and jeans. "It's brisk out there," she said. "Aren't you cold?"

He shook his head. "These temperatures don't bother me."

"Well, *I'm* cold. You must be hot-blooded."

Adam's mouth quirked. Realizing what she'd said, Jenny blushed. "Coffee?"

"If it's no trouble."

"None at all. Make yourself comfortable. I'll be right back."

When she returned with the coffee and a plate of store-bought gingersnaps, Adam was standing before the curio shelf. She set his mug and the plate on her tidy coffee table.

"You own some nice pieces." He nodded at the sculpture of the teacher and child. "I especially like that one."

"Thanks. My father gave it to me when I earned my teaching degree."

"Is he a teacher, too?"

"He was a principal. He died last year," Jenny said, her voice remarkably steady, considering she'd lost not only her beloved father, but also her fiancé, and life as she'd known it.

"I'm sorry."

Adam's compassionate expression spoke volumes. He understood the pain of losing a loved one, but that didn't mean Jenny was about to explain about her other losses.

"I lost my dad six years ago," he said. "Two years later, Mom died."

"Having lost both parents, too, I know how difficult that is."

Not wanting any questions about her mother, Jenny quickly added, "You've lost a lot of people in a short time."

"Just about everyone I love. If it weren't for Abby, I don't know how—" Looking taken aback at what he'd just revealed, Adam abruptly cut himself off, his mouth an angry slash.

Jenny started to reach out a comforting hand. Remembering what had happened the last time she'd touched him, she settled for words, instead. "I'm so sorry, Ad—"

"I don't want your pity."

His pain-filled gaze bored into hers, then darted away.

"Okay." Jenny swallowed. "Your coffee's getting cold, and you came here to talk about Abby," she said. "Please, sit down."

Adam gave a terse nod and dropped onto the armchair. Tension radiated from him, so much so that Jenny's stomach twisted in knots.

Tonight wasn't turning out at all as she'd imagined. Wishing she could start the evening all over again, she sat down on the sofa.

SILENTLY KICKING HIMSELF, Adam took a long pull on his coffee. He didn't talk about himself or his problems. Ever. Yet tonight he'd all but shared his most private thoughts with Jenny. Thank God he'd come to his senses and shut his mouth in time.

Not soon enough. Her pitying look had slashed right through him, making him feel as weak as a newborn calf. When he was anything but and needed no one.

No trace of pity in her eyes now. Perched on the edge of the sofa in the skirt and blouse she'd probably taught in, her hands locked together in her lap and her legs pinched together, she looked acutely uncomfortable. Adam breathed a sigh of relief. This was so much better than having her feel sorry for him.

On the heels of his relief, he felt like a jerk for being short with her, especially when she was giving up her evening to discuss Abby. "Where's your coffee?" he asked in an effort to make nice.

"I don't drink it after mid-afternoon, otherwise the caffeine keeps me up all hours." She almost smiled. "I gather you don't have that problem."

Better, much better. "Never have." He grabbed a gingersnap, then passed the plate to Jenny. She shook her head.

"I work too hard to lie awake nights for anything," he said, not wanting her thinking his grief kept him up at night. It didn't, not anymore. Realizing how bad that sounded, he added, "Not that you don't work hard, too."

"Teaching is taxing in a different way. Your job is more physical. You're getting ready to winter some of your cattle, sell others and wean the calves from their mothers, am I right?"

Astonished, Adam gaped at her. "Among other things. How'd you know that?"

"From a program I heard on the radio. This must be your busiest time of year."

"When you run a ranch, every time of year is busy except for a few months in the deep of winter."

"I never realized. But then, I don't know much about cattle ranching."

"So you said that first day we met. Any time you want to learn, stop by, and I'll show you around."

Adam couldn't believe his own words. Had he just invited Jenny to the ranch? Of all the crazy things to do.

"I just might do that."

She was relaxed now, her face full of light and energy. What would she look like in the throes of passion?

The urge to pull her onto his lap and kiss her was so strong, his groin stirred. He itched to cut and run. And he would, as soon as she told him about Abby.

Adam propped his arms on his thighs and cleared his throat. "Abby's been in school a full week now, and I haven't seen much of a change in her." He didn't expect miracles, but he'd hoped for a glimmer of improvement.

Both Megan and Mrs. Ames reported that every afternoon Abby trudged into the house, tired and sullen, unhappy. Adam had no idea how to fix her problems and never had. It was a helpless feeling he detested.

"How is she doing at school?" he asked.

"Some things take time. Learning and change happens at a child's own pace. With Abby, we're talking baby steps. She *is* listening in class, and that's a positive." Pausing, Jenny smoothed down her skirt and bit her lip. "Everyone is trying hard to make her feel comfortable and accepted."

Adam tore his gaze from her sexy mouth. "Everyone?"

"The other students and I. We all want to see Abby involved and happy."

"You said you'd make a plan to help her."

"I know I did."

"Where the hell is it?"

Jenny bristled. "I don't appreciate your tone."

Instantly Adam regretted his sharpness. "I, uh, guess I'm a little impatient," he said by way of apologizing. "I know you're doing your best. Is there something I can do?"

The starch went out of her spine. "Hide that impatience from Abby. Let her know you love her no matter what."

Jenny must think he was an insensitive jerk. Adam gave

a terse nod. Unable to sit for one more second, he stood and began to pace. Or tried. In the little room, he was lucky to take three steps before he was forced to turn around.

"I visited Miss Graham last Friday," Jenny said.

"My old teacher?" He pivoted and moved toward her. "What for?"

"Because I'm out of my league here, and I needed her advice."

Adam appreciated Jenny's honesty. He also respected the teacher he'd had from kindergarten through eighth grade, who knew plenty about kids and what they needed from school. He veered toward the oak kitchen table. "What'd she say?"

"Do you mind holding still? The pacing is distracting."

Adam crossed his arms and canted his hips against the front door. Which was as far as he could get from Jenny and still be in the same room.

"She sent her regards," Jenny said. "And she told me a funny story about you."

"Funny?"

Her lips twitched. "About the time you stole all her chalk and she had nothing to write with."

"When she figured out it was me, I sure wasn't laughing. She made me scrub the blackboard every day for weeks." Remembering, Adam grinned. "Which I deserved. Back then, I was a real smart-ass."

"You were a teenager."

"Same difference."

Jenny chuckled, then for the first time tonight, smiled her full-on, dazzling smile. Adam realized he'd been waiting for that, and it made him mad. He didn't want to have feelings for Jenny. He was here for his child.

"What else did Miss Graham say?" he asked more gruffly

than he'd intended. Jenny's eyes narrowed. Dreading another teacherly rebuke about his tone, he softened his voice. "About Abby."

"She mentioned the daughter of a friend, a speech therapist named Carla Jenson, who might be able to help."

"A speech therapist for Abby." Adam scratched his head. "That makes about as much sense as sending a paraplegic to dance lessons."

"This is an entirely different situation, Adam. What if Abby is capable of talking? We won't know if we don't try. This afternoon, I took the liberty of contacting Mrs. Jenson, and she's eager to meet Abby. She's holding an appointment time for you on Friday afternoon, and would like you to call and confirm. Here's her number."

Jenny held out a stickie, forcing Adam to move closer. She placed it in his hand, her fingers a sweet brush of heat against his palm.

"Friday? That's the day after tomorrow. Awful short notice."

"True, but we're lucky she had an open slot. There is one more thing. She isn't local. Her office is in the town of Red Deer."

Of all the places in Montana… Adam frowned.

"Is that bad?" Jenny asked.

It was when your occasional bed partner lived there. Adam didn't like the idea of bringing his daughter to the town where they might run into Sheila. He shook his head. "I don't have the time to change the oil in my truck, let alone drive out there regularly. Besides, this whole thing could be a bust, and I don't want my daughter hurt with false hope."

Jenny sighed. "I understand, Adam, but we have to try. This woman comes highly recommended. She deserves a chance to help Abby. Could Megan take her?"

"She has chores of her own. Plus she already drives Abby to and from school every day. That's enough."

Jenny huffed an impatient breath. "I know you're busy, Adam, but Abby needs extra help." Her plump lips became a thin, stubborn line.

Why that was sexy was any fool's guess.

A growing desire for Jenny, worry over Abby, fatigue—all of it shortened Adam's fuse.

Better mad than lust-filled, and he grabbed on to his anger like a lifeline. If his tone offended her, tough. "You don't know anything. You have one hell of a nerve, butting in where you don't belong."

Jenny's back stiffened. She stood and faced him. "I am not butting in—Abby is my student, and that gives me every right to offer help and assistance."

"Fine. Now back off."

"You are the most exasperating man!" She thrust out her chin, and narrowed her eyes, which sparked with temper.

Damned if Adam didn't want to kiss her more than ever. He backed away until the door stopped him.

Jenny followed him the whole way, just about sticking her nose in his face. "This is your daughter we're talking about! Make. The. Time."

"I'm not one of your students. You do not get to order me around," Adam warned, upping the scowl that intimidated people and pushed them away.

Not Jenny. Unlike everyone else, she held her ground, never giving an inch. "I'm trying to help, you stubborn lug!"

God above, she was sexy. "There's no cause for name-calling."

"There is when the name fits."

"Point taken. Okay, I'll get her there on Friday." He pushed a strand of incredibly soft hair off her face, and tucked it behind her ear.

Her eyes darkened. "Wh-what are you doing?" she asked, her voice whispering across his skin like a caress.

Adam lost the fight to keep his distance. Stepping closer, he cupped her head between his hands. "Getting ready to kiss you."

Chapter Six

Jenny felt so damned good in Adam's arms, much better than any fantasy. And lately he'd enjoyed plenty of those. Sighing, she twined her arms around his neck so that her soft breasts pillowed on his chest.

Her lips tasted sweet and welcoming. Eager. He hadn't kissed a woman in a long time, had never enjoyed a kiss quite so much. Or caught fire so fast. Heat flared and burned through him like dry tinder struck by lightning.

All too soon, Jenny unwrapped her arms from his neck. Adam wanted to pull her close again. He changed his mind when she placed her hands on his chest.

They slid lower. His hungry body hardened with need, and his mind all but blanked. Desire surged through him. To lie down with her, right here on the rug. Wrap her legs around his hips and—

"Stop, Adam."

Instead of moving her palms downward, she was trying to shove him away. Jerking him from his haze of need.

What in God's name was he doing?

He let go of her, and she hastily stepped back. Her hair was messy, her cheeks flushed, and her lips moist and red.

From his kisses. She was so damned sexy. And this was wrong in so many ways.

"I'm sorry, Jenny. I—" He broke off, scrubbed his face. "I was out of line."

Yet true as that was, he wanted to kiss her again. And more.

Looking dazed, she nodded. He waited for her to tell him off, but she didn't say a word, and her silence made him feel even worse.

"I had no call to yell at you earlier," he went on. "Abby's problems aren't your fault—they're mine." For not knowing how to coax her to speak, for everything that had happened since before and after her birth. "You were right to contact that speech therapist. First thing tomorrow I'll call her. Good night."

He slipped out the door, pulling it shut behind him.

As soon as the rumble of Adam's truck faded away, Jenny sank onto the armchair. The smell of his aftershave surrounded her, as if it had penetrated the fabric of the chair. She inhaled deeply, then caught herself.

"We only shared a few kisses," she assured herself. Very long, delicious kisses. "Nothing to worry about."

Jumping up, she stacked Adam's mug on the empty cookie plate and carried both to the kitchen. She managed to wash the dishes and coffeepot before her thoughts spun back to what had happened tonight.

Adam had kissed her, and she'd let him. No, that wasn't quite right. She'd more than allowed his kisses—she'd participated. With enthusiasm.

She'd thoroughly enjoyed every moment. His muscled arms holding her close. The strength of his lean, hard body. His mouth on hers, awakening and stirring dangerous feelings.

Physical desire and the undeniable longing for connection on a deeper level. Scary.

Jenny's body and her parched spirit ached to be with Adam. Her rational mind shuddered.

She could not, would not, get romantically involved with Adam Dawson. Not when she was here only through the end of the school year. Besides, no sane man would want a serious relationship with the daughter of a schizophrenic. Rob hadn't. Once he'd learned the truth, he'd treated her like a pariah.

No doubt Adam would, too. Therefore, she would never let him know her secret.

Adam Dawson was Abby's father, and Jenny was Abby's teacher. Period. There would be no more kisses. Ever.

Satisfied that this was the right thing to do, Jenny finished the dishes and dried her hands.

At least some good had come of the evening—Adam had agreed to contact Carla Jenson.

Suddenly his parting words filled her mind. "Abby's problems aren't your fault—they're mine."

Jenny puzzled over that. No one held Adam responsible for his daughter's failure to speak, yet he seemed to. Why?

FRIDAY AFTERNOON, ADAM picked up Abby after school to take her to the appointment in Red Deer. After what had happened the other night he dreaded facing Jenny. At least he didn't have to do it alone, as other parents were also picking up their kids.

Adam greeted them. He noted how the kids called out goodbyes to one another. Without fail, every one of them included Abby. If she couldn't speak, she could've waved or smiled. But no, she simply chewed her lip and hung her head.

Seeing her so dejected just about killed Adam. With all his heart and soul, he hoped for a miracle, that Carla Jenson would somehow help his little girl.

"Hey, there," he said, helping her into her Windbreaker.

He nodded at Jenny who stood nearby. She smiled brightly, but her eyes didn't smile. Her gaze was impersonal, glancing off him, as if she'd never wrapped her arms around his neck or pressed close and kissed him back.

As if she was Abby's teacher, nothing more.

Which was exactly what Adam wanted and how things should be. Now, if he could just forget how she tasted, could stop this crazy wanting that had only increased since the other night…

Her outfit didn't help. The pale yellow dress showcased her slender waist and round hips, and showed a nice stretch of leg. Neither did that shiny, light brown hair, one stubborn lock falling into her eye. Adam wanted to tuck it behind her ear, but touching her was dangerous.

"Let me know how the appointment goes," she said, directing an encouraging smile at Abby.

"You want me to call and tell you about it?" Adam asked. Father to a teacher.

Looking panicky, Jenny shook her head. "Um, that's okay. I'm sure I'll hear about it later."

Maybe she was afraid to talk to him without other people around. He was right there with her.

"Hey, Adam," a woman behind him cooed. "Are you bringing Drew and Megan with you tomorrow night?"

Tomorrow night? He turned to greet Anita Eden, a busybody who'd gone to school with him. She'd chased after him then, and after her divorce, she'd started up again, always flirting. Not interested. He frowned.

"At the Prairie Community Center?" she went on. "The potluck and dance for our Miss Wyler." She smiled at Jenny.

Adam had nearly forgotten about that. He'd have preferred to avoid seeing Jenny over the weekend, but he couldn't get out of an evening held in her honor without stirring up a hornet's nest of questions and curiosity.

"We'll all be there." He tapped his daughter's shoulder. "Let's go, Abby, or we'll be late."

Megan had tossed Brianna in the back beside the booster seat. As soon as Abby buckled herself in, she snatched up the doll.

"Here's your snack." Adam handed her the fat brown bag Mrs. Ames had packed. "It's a lot of food," he said, "because we might not get home until past dinnertime."

By the time Adam pulled out of the school lot, Abby was biting into her cheese sandwich.

Her obvious appetite was a step up from what it had been since that first day of school. That was a good sign, right? Baby steps, Jenny had said the other night.

But when Adam glanced in the rearview mirror a moment later, most of the sandwich remained intact. His suddenly pale daughter was holding Brianna in a death grip and staring out the window.

So much for baby steps.

"Miss Wyler thinks that Mrs. Jenson can help you," he said over his shoulder. "But I never asked—do you want that help?"

Abby nodded, but still looked worried.

Adam worried, too. He was also wary. What if this so-called expert turned out to be like the other two?

He wasn't about to share his misgivings. "When I talked with Mrs. Jenson on the phone yesterday, she sounded a lot different than those two people we saw last year. I think we should give her a chance."

Carla Jenson had seemed kind, a good match for Abby, and had laid out what would happen in their first forty-five-minute meeting. "Most of the time, I won't be in the room. It'll just be you and Mrs. Jenson," Adam explained, glancing in the mirror again to gauge his daughter's reaction.

She seemed okay with that. "If you don't like her, we don't have to come back," he added.

Adam intended to use the time by stopping at the bar and telling Sheila he wouldn't be coming to see her again. He doubted she'd mind, but felt he owed her the courtesy of letting her know.

Carla Jenson's office turned out to be around the corner and down the block from the Red Deer Tavern. Too far away to be seen by Sheila, if she happened to be in there and glanced out the window. Not wanting to tempt fate, though, Adam ducked his head, cupped Abby's shoulder, and hustled her inside.

The reception area–waiting room wasn't much bigger than Abby's bedroom. There was no one at the reception desk.

"Hello?" Adam called out.

Abby stayed close by his side, her nervousness almost palpable.

"I'll be right there."

A fifty-something woman entered the room. With her gray-streaked, wiry hair twisted into a messy bun, and a loose blouse and slacks, she looked like somebody's grandma.

"Sorry about that. My receptionist leaves at three-thirty when her kids get home from school." She offered a warm smile. "You must be Adam and Abby. I'm Carla Jenson—you may call me Miss Carla, Abby."

They shook hands. The speech therapist had a firm, confident grip.

"Here are those papers I mentioned." Adam handed her copies of the same reports he'd given Jenny.

"Thanks. Please, come into my office."

Adam and Abby followed her into a room crowded with a desk, computer, a file cabinet and shelves of books. Two diplomas hung on the wall, one declaring her a Phi Beta Kappa.

Impressive but Adam would wait and see. A new folder lay on the desktop; Abby's name was on it.

"This is where I do my paperwork and so forth. There's another room for the children I work with. It's a pretty special place, just for kids. I'm the only grown-up allowed in there. Would you like to see it, Abby?"

Abby shot Adam a nervous look. "It's okay," he said.

The speech therapist waited for his daughter's nod before opening a door at the back of the room.

Adam glimpsed a brightly colored space, filled with child-size furniture, books and toys.

"Go on in and look around, honey, while your daddy and I chat," Carla said. "Then if you don't mind, I'll send him away for a little while, so that you and I can work by ourselves. How does that sound?"

This time, Abby didn't so much as glance at Adam for his okay. She simply nodded.

Ten minutes later, he entered the tavern. At this time of day, only a handful of patrons were at the bar. Adam squinted in the dim light. The smells of whisky and stale smoke assaulted his nose.

"Is Sheila here?" he asked the bartender.

The beefy male eyed him. "Why?"

"I, uh, wanted to give her a message."

"Can't help you, bud. She quit. Got married and moved to Missoula."

Relieved, Adam smiled. "That's great news."

Whistling, he returned to the waiting room. He spent the next twenty minutes leafing through well-thumbed magazines.

When Carla delivered Abby to the waiting room, his daughter seemed relaxed. He raised his eyebrows at her, and she skipped toward him.

"Looks like you two had a good time," he said.

Carla nodded. "We did. For the first few months or so, I need to see Abby twice a week."

"We live in Saddlers Prairie, and I'm a rancher," Adam explained. With fence still to mend, and cattle to vaccinate and herd before winter.

"My father was a rancher, so believe me, I understand, Mr. Dawson—Adam. But seeing your daughter twice a week for a while is imperative." She turned to Abby, her face kind. "I know I can teach you to talk. But you have to want to, and you must work hard, both with me, at school and at home."

Words Adam had never expected to hear. Hope surged through him. "How do you feel about that, Abby?"

Suddenly, his daughter did something extraordinary. She grinned.

With that, he made up his mind. Traveling to Red Deer twice a week wasn't going to be easy or convenient, but for Abby's sake, he'd figure out a way.

Chapter Seven

After an enjoyable Skype session with Becca Saturday afternoon, Jenny dressed for the potluck and dance. Minutes after she pulled onto the highway, the wind kicked up, and a torrential downpour pummeled the car. She drove at a snail's pace, gripping the wheel to counter the wind gusts trying to push the car off the highway. Seattle had its share of rain, but nothing like this.

According to the locals, the Prairie Community Center, which served several towns in the area, was just off the highway and easy to find. Jenny hoped so, because even with the wipers on high, visibility was only about five feet ahead.

At least with her focus totally on arriving in one piece, the anxieties about the evening ahead faded into the background. The spotlight would be on her at the beginning of the evening, but with a live band and dancing, Jenny figured the attention would be short-lived. She wanted to fit in, not stand out. Then, as soon as good manners allowed, she'd leave.

The brightly lit building was easy to spot from the highway. As Jenny pulled into the parking lot, she blew out a breath. Made it. Now to survive the evening.

Cars and trucks filled the slots closest to the door. No umbrella could stand up to this wind, and Jenny was glad for her hooded jacket. As she dashed for the door, a cold gust whipped the hood back. Shivering, she pushed through the entrance.

Anita Eden sat at a card table, checking in guests. She smiled when she saw Jenny. "There you are. With the storm, we were worried you missed the turnoff."

"You gave great directions. It's awful out there! It doesn't rain like this in Seattle."

"We usually don't get rain like this, either. Not for another few weeks yet. It probably won't last. The coatrack is over there." Anita gestured to one side. "If you want to comb your hair, the restroom is around the corner. I'm waiting on a few more people, then I'll see you inside."

When Jenny checked herself in the bathroom mirror, she knew why Anita had suggested she stop there—her hair was a flyaway mess. She didn't want anyone seeing her like this. Especially Adam.

Was he here yet? Jenny hoped so. She wanted to hear how Abby's appointment went yesterday. She imagined him studying her with the dark intensity that all but ruined her concentration. The look that made her want things from him. Things she couldn't have.

Stern-faced, she pulled a lipstick from her purse. "Adam is Abby's father, period," she said. Ever since their kiss, this had been her mantra.

Determined to remember that tonight, she entered the assembly hall with her nerves humming. The bright fluorescent lights overhead, the buffed wood floor and yellow cinderblock walls reminded her of a high-school gym, which was almost reassuring.

The sea of people was not.

Fighting the urge to turn around and go home, she hovered just inside the door. No one had noticed her yet, and conversation and laughter bubbled around her. If only she could stay here, unobserved all evening.

Looking for a familiar face, she searched the room for Adam. She didn't see him, but there were plenty of other faces she knew. Others she didn't recognize. She was sure that would change soon.

Someone had hung a huge hand-printed banner high on one wall that proclaimed Welcome, Miss Wyler.

The two long tables beneath the banner were loaded with food Jenny suspected was home-cooked. Her stomach gurgled. Nervous about tonight, she hadn't eaten since lunch.

At the end of one table, she spotted Val and Silas setting out a platter. Val waved and beckoned her over.

"Well, don't you look pretty," she said. "That soft peach color brings out the roses in your cheeks. Or is that from the wind?"

"What's it matter, Val?" Silas said. "Either way, she's a good-lookin' gal."

"Thanks. What a lovely party." Jenny swallowed. "There sure are a lot of people here tonight."

"Just about the whole town—at least those who could make it," Val said. "We're all so glad you decided to teach here. Wait till the band arrives and the dancing starts. Ranchers don't get out much, especially this time of year. When they do, they make the most of it. What with the storm and all, we picked one heck of a night to welcome you to town. I just hope the power doesn't go out."

"That reminds me," Silas said. "If you ever lose power in the cottage, there's a gas generator in that shed out back. You'll want to keep a gas can filled and at the ready."

"That's good to know," Jenny said. "Does the power go out often?"

Before Silas could reply, Barb joined them. "There you are, Jenny. Anita said you were here. A whole bunch of people want to meet you. Come on, I'll introduce you around." She exchanged sly looks with Val—what did that mean?—then fluttered her fingers goodbye and directed Jenny toward a small knot of men.

Only one was close to Jenny's age. The rest looked to be at least twenty years older.

Barb hooked her arm through Jenny's and brought her into the group. "Meet Jenny Wyler, our lovely and competent teacher. You know my other half." She patted Emilio's arm, then gestured at a roundish, balding male. "This is Dr. Tom, the man to see if you need any kind of medical treatment. If you ever go to court, you'll meet up with Judge Neimeyer, the tall, eagle-eyed fella with the silver handlebar moustache. Next to him is Phil Covey, one of our more successful cattle ranchers who lives on the edge of town. His young, handsome friend, the one with all his hair, is Cody Naylor."

The name sounded vaguely familiar, but Jenny couldn't recall where she'd heard it.

Barb covered her mouth, but failed to lower her voice. "Cody is the single fella I mentioned that day you arrived in town."

Now Jenny understood the sly look. She blushed, and Cody gave her a what-can-you-do shrug.

She also met the town banker, the Realtor, and the insurance agent, his wife and four-year-old twins.

Students and their parents wandered over to say hello, and Barb, Emilio and the other men slipped away. Jenny met aunts, uncles, grandparents, cousins and siblings. Nervous as she was, everyone was beyond nice, and she thought she might actually survive the evening.

All the while, she searched for Adam, but she didn't see him, Abby or Megan. He'd said they'd be here, but maybe he'd changed his mind.

Jenny told herself she didn't care, but disappointment cut sharply through her.

"Looking for someone?" Val asked.

Not wanting her personal business broadcast through the crowd, Jenny shook her head. "Just taking in all these people. I had no idea—"

Suddenly Barb tapped the microphone attached to the small podium at the front of the room. By the loud *thump* the mic was definitely working.

"Evening, everyone," she said. "Thanks for coming, and thanks for bringing your best dishes to welcome Miss Jenny Wyler, our new teacher here in Saddlers Prairie. Anytime now, the band should arrive, and if I were you, I'd grab dinner before the dancing starts. For those of you who haven't met Miss Wyler, please introduce yourself. She's been teaching our kids for two weeks now, and parents and kids are raving about her. Would you like to say hello, Miss Wyler?"

No one had mentioned speaking. The butterflies flooded back, along with the urge to flee. But people were glancing Jenny's way, shooting her expectant looks. There was no way out of this except to get it over with.

On legs that held remarkably steady, Jenny made her way to the podium.

"I didn't know I'd be standing up here, and I'm not exactly prepared. But being a teacher, I always have something to say." As she'd hoped, people laughed. "Teaching in a one-room school is not without its challenges. It's harder than it looks. A *lot* harder." More laughter. "As Barb said, we just finished our second week. Without a doubt, this is the most enthusiastic group of students I've ever had the privilege of teaching. We're off to a good start, and I expect we'll have a great year. Thanks for coming tonight."

Amid whoops and applause, she stepped away from the mic with a sigh of relief. She was moving away from the podium when the main door opened.

Megan Dawson entered the room, holding hands with a tall male who bore a striking resemblance to Adam. An older woman with short hair and glasses followed behind. Large casserole in hand, she headed for the food tables. Abby had come, too, but Jenny's attention settled on Adam.

As always, he was breathtakingly handsome. Tonight he'd exchanged the usual T-shirt and jeans for an oxford shirt, a sports coat and dark slacks.

Jenny knew exactly when he noticed her. His gaze caught hers and held. The funny, fluttery feeling she was getting used to whenever he was near filled her insides.

People clustered around her, and she managed to participate in the conversation. The whole time, though, she was keenly aware of Adam making his way through the crowd. Toward her.

She didn't want to feel giddy, didn't want to care that he was here. That she did unsettled her, and for a moment she considered pretending she hadn't noticed him and walking away in the opposite direction.

But she could no more turn from his intent gaze than stop breathing.

JENNY WAS EASY TO SPOT, her dress a splash of pale pink in a sea of blues and blacks. With her lively expression and that straight, shiny hair almost brushing her shoulders, she was hands down the most beautiful woman in the room.

Adam swallowed. Hardly aware of what he was doing, he headed toward her.

As if she felt his stare, she glanced at him. Even from across the room, her face telegraphed her feelings as clearly as any words.

She was glad to see him.

Anticipation quickened his pace. Only because he was eager to tell her about Abby's appointment yesterday, he assured himself.

The people milling around Jenny made room for him in

the circle. Adam nodded a hello, then ignored them. "I'm told we missed your speech, and I apologize," he said.

"That's okay. I didn't have anything planned, and really didn't say much."

She wouldn't quite meet his eyes, and her smile seemed halfhearted. The warm look that had drawn him to her had vanished like dust in the rain, making him wonder if he'd imagined it. She sure didn't seem pleased that he was standing here.

"See you later, Jenny," someone in the group said.

Everyone ambled off. Except Adam.

Jenny was no help. She said nothing. He stood there like a damned fool, racking his brain for a topic of conversation.

Luckily Mrs. Ames showed up with Abby.

"Goodness, Adam, you took off so fast, you left the rest of us back by the door. Hello, Miss Wyler, I'm Mrs. Ames, the housekeeper at Dawson Ranch. I've been looking forward to this all week. It's a real pleasure to meet Abby's teacher."

"Please, call me Jenny. It's nice to meet you, too." Jenny turned to Abby, her expression shifting subtly, softening and gentling. "Hello, Abby. I like your party dress."

Abby nodded, then glanced down, but Adam thought he saw the corners of her mouth lift.

Baby steps.

"How's our Abby doing in school?" Mrs. Ames asked.

"I'm awfully glad to see her every morning," Jenny said.

The reply was guaranteed to make his daughter feel good. Clearly it worked, for Abby's back straightened a fraction. Adam silently thanked Jenny.

She raised one eyebrow slightly, and he knew she was curious about yesterday's appointment. He wanted to tell her about it, but not in front of Abby or Mrs. Ames, even though they both knew exactly what he did.

"We're glad you came to Saddlers Prairie," his housekeeper was saying. "You're just what the school needed—especially Abby." She gave Adam's daughter a grandmotherly pat.

"That's nice to hear." Jenny glanced at Adam, as if wanting him to take note.

"I wouldn't say it if it wasn't true. Abby likes going to school, and that's because of you. We were so worried she wouldn't. Shall we get something to eat, Abby?" She took the little hand and they headed for the food tables.

"Mrs. Ames seems nice," Jenny said.

Adam nodded. "She's been with us thirty-three years, since I was a newborn."

"That long. Wow, that's impressive. I'll bet she knows a few stories about you that rival Miss Graham's."

"She does, but she's smart enough to keep them to herself." He couldn't help chuckling, which cut the tension.

"What happened at the appointment yesterday?" she asked.

He was about to tell her when Megan and Drew sauntered over.

"Hi," Jenny said, brightening up, as warm and welcoming toward them as he wished she'd be to him.

Not anymore. He was on the outside now, and sorry for it. All because of those kisses.

"—My husband, Drew," Megan was saying. "Adam's younger brother."

"I thought so." Jenny glanced from Adam to Drew. "There's a definite resemblance between you two."

"I've seen the family photo albums," Megan said. "They both have the strong Wyler jaw and sky-blue eyes." She winked. "But Drew's the best-looking."

Her husband grinned. "You'd better think so." He held out his hand. "Pleasure to meet you, Jenny. Megan's been talking about you nonstop. She's real happy you joined her book club."

Megan gave an enthusiastic nod. "Once winter hits and things slow down at the ranch, I'm planning on inviting you over for dinner."

Adam had also invited Jenny to the ranch. Sooner or later she'd probably visit. For some reason he wanted her to see the ranch that belonged to him and Drew. He wasn't about to examine why.

Wanting Drew and Megan gone, he said nothing during the chitchat that followed. Soon enough, his brother and sister-in-law got the message.

"I'm hungry, Drew. Let's get something to eat." Megan tugged on her husband's arm. "See you both later."

Once again, Adam had Jenny to himself. Not sure where to start, he rocked back on his heels. Blew out a breath. Shoved his hands into his pants pockets. "Look, Jenny, I—"

"Why don't you—" Jenny said at the same time.

"You go first," Adam said.

"That's okay, really."

"Please, go ahead."

"I was only going to ask if you'd eaten yet," she said.

"Just a bite earlier this afternoon." Not nearly enough. Adam was running on empty. "You?"

She shook her head. "Too nervous."

"You, nervous? About what?"

"I'm not exactly comfortable around all these people, and I really don't like the attention."

"Are you kidding? I've been watching you, and you're great with everyone." *Way to go, Dawson. Why not broadcast the fact you've been staring at her.* Adam cleared his throat. "Heck, you teach. You're always the center of attention."

"It's different with kids. They don't ju—they're more accepting. The Seattle School District would never throw a welcome-to-the-district party like this, especially for just one teacher."

"We're a small town. They're a big city."

"You can say that again."

Did she regret coming here? Adam couldn't tell. "Do you miss Seattle?" he asked.

"No," she answered without hesitation. Shadows filled her eyes.

Adam wondered what put them there, but that wasn't his business. He had enough ghosts of his own.

"We're both hungry. Why don't we grab ourselves some food and find a place to sit? While we eat, I'll tell you about Abby's appointment yesterday."

"That sounds good."

Rather than walking beside him, Jenny made a beeline for the tables. Adam followed behind her. He started to place his hand on the small of her back, then changed his mind.

Suddenly the side door opened, and four men dressed in Western shirts, Stetsons, jeans and cowboy boots filed into the room. Two carried guitars, one lugged a base. They headed for the drum set someone had set up where the podium had stood.

As the musicians tuned their instruments, people wandered toward them. Jenny slowed, letting Adam catch up to her. "Apparently the dance is about to start," she said.

"Looks like it. That ought to clear out the crowd around the food."

"Val says that ranchers don't get out much this time of year. She says you're usually too busy to socialize."

Adam nodded. "Too much to do before winter, so I probably shouldn't be here."

From the look on her face, he realized how his comment sounded. "I'm not sorry I'm here," he backtracked. "I only meant that because of the work, I can't stay long tonight."

They were about five feet from the food table when the band's mic squeaked.

"All right, folks." The lead singer's voice boomed through the room. "Grab your sweethearts, and come on out to the dance floor, 'cause it's time to boogie."

Everyone seemed to pair up—kids, too. Mrs. Ames even coaxed Abby to the dance area.

Adam shifted around and scratched the back of his neck. Out of the corners of his eye, he saw that Jenny was looking at the band, her hands folded at her waist, a smile glued to her mouth.

Nearby, Val and Silas tossed their plates into the trash, then started toward the dance area.

"Aren't you two going to dance?" Val asked as they passed by.

Adam shrugged. "That's up to Jenny."

"Um, okay. Sure."

He couldn't read her expression, but decided to take advantage of the opportunity. He may not be able to kiss her again, but it didn't mean they couldn't be friends. At least for Abby's sake.

Adam took her hand and led her toward the band.

Chapter Eight

Couples whirled and spun around Adam and Jenny, showing off all kinds of fancy steps. Adam stuck with what he knew—the waltz.

"One winter, my mom taught me how to dance," he said. "She was pretty good, but I'm not."

"Just don't step on my toes, and we'll be fine," Jenny said with a smile.

Adam dipped his head and got lost in the flowery smell of her hair. "I haven't had a chance to tell you how pretty you look tonight," he murmured.

The color rose in her cheeks. "Thanks. You look good, too. I've never seen you in slacks and a sports coat."

"I don't like wearing dress clothes, but now and then, a man has to wear something other than jeans."

He waltzed her around, Jenny nestling against him as if she belonged.

"You were going to tell me about yesterday," she said.

Adam's senses were so full of her scent and her soft warmth, that it took a moment for him to decipher what she wanted to know.

"The appointment went pretty well. Abby seemed comfortable, and Mrs. Jenson treated her like you do—with warmth and friendly respect."

"Why, Adam, what a sweet thing to say about me—and Carla."

Jenny's glowing expression made him feel as if he'd won the lottery. "It's true," he said, smiling.

"And? What did she say about Abby?"

"She says she thinks she can teach her to talk, with help from you and me."

"Oh, Adam. That's wonderful!"

Jenny laughed, a sweet, lilting sound that settled like a song in his chest. She was so happy for Abby and so beautiful. And she was in his arms. *His*—at least for this dance. Adam pulled her a little closer.

Several people glanced their way, but he paid them no attention. "I owe you an apology, Jenny, for telling you to butt out when you were trying to do right for Abby."

"Apology accepted. Tomorrow, I'll call Phylinda Graham and thank her for the referral. Then Monday during recess, I'll call Carla and find out what she'd like me to do."

"That'd be good. She's planning to give Abby a list of things to practice at home. She also wants to see her twice a week for a few months."

Jenny frowned. "With so much to do at the ranch, how will you manage that?"

"I haven't figured that part out yet." He didn't want to ask Megan, but this was too important, he didn't have much choice.

"I'll drive her one day a week, if you like."

Outside of immediate family, and then only when absolutely necessary, Adam didn't like accepting favors from people. He shook his head. "You've already done enough for us."

"I don't mind, Adam. Besides it's only for a month or two, right?"

"I can't let you do that."

"Yes, you can. Just nod your head and say, 'Okay, Jenny. Thanks.' Go ahead, try it."

With her eyes sparkling, she was impossible to resist. Adam laughed. "Okay, Jenny. Thanks."

"See? That wasn't so hard."

"I'll figure out a way to pay you back."

"Having Abby happy and able to speak will be plenty of payback."

"We'll see about that."

He wanted to hug her, wanted to kiss her so badly, he ached. But he'd lost that easy warmth once and he wasn't about to make that mistake again. Besides, he'd promised, and the last thing he wanted to do was alienate Jenny from him when she was helping so much with Abby.

Somebody tapped him on the shoulder. Adam glanced around to find Cody Naylor flashing his toothy grin.

He was Adam's age and about the same height. He'd just moved back to town to take care of Phil Covey, the man who'd raised him as a son, after Phil was diagnosed with terminal cancer. Cody was a decent enough guy. Also smart and richer than sin. Women everywhere loved him; Jenny probably would, too.

"Mind if I cut in?" Naylor asked.

Adam definitely minded, but Jenny was already smiling at the guy. Reluctantly, Adam let her go.

He watched from the sidelines as Naylor swept Jenny around the floor in ways Adam could never match. The two of them talking and enjoying each other's company.

Adam didn't like the interested look on Naylor's face. He felt tense, as if he wanted to punch someone.

Drew and Megan stopped dancing to catch their breaths. Drew glanced from Adam to Jenny and Naylor, then back to Adam. "Huh," he said.

Adam glared at him. "Huh, what?"

Drew put his hands up. "I didn't say anything. You haven't eaten yet, have you? Why don't you fix yourself a plate. Filling your belly should improve your mood dramatically."

"Not hungry."

Heading again to the dance area, Adam weaved his way through the dancers. He tapped Naylor's shoulder none too gently.

"Ouch," Cody said.

Hiking his thumb behind them, Adam gestured him away. "My turn."

JENNY BARELY CAUGHT HER BREATH before Adam pulled her into his arms and waltzed her around.

"Hello, again. I thought you hated dancing."

"I never said that. I said I wasn't any good at it. Not smooth, like Cody Naylor." He guided her toward the outer edge of the dance floor. "Trust me, he's not your type."

She looked at him, and tried to ignore the warmth she felt in his arms. "Just how would you know that?"

"Call it instinct."

"Thanks for the warning, but FYI, though Cody seems nice, I'm not interested in him."

When she felt Adam relax suddenly, she realized she needed to set things straight. "I'm recently out of a relationship, and I'm not ready to date."

"What happened?" Adam asked. "Not that your love life is any of my business."

"I really don't feel like talking about it." Afraid of more questions, Jenny started to pull out of his arms.

"That's okay by me," he said without letting her go. "We haven't finished our conversation about Abby, and I swear my belly's so empty, that my ribs are sticking to my backbone. We both need to eat. Let's get dinner and take it into the hall, where we can hear ourselves think."

He was right about needing food. Jenny was beyond starving, almost light-headed. Discussing Abby over dinner sounded safe enough. "Okay," she said.

As famished as she was, she limited herself to one fried chicken thigh, a roll and a generous helping of green salad, while Adam piled his plate with chicken, several kinds of casserole, cornbread, salad and three buttered rolls. A mountain of food. He was a big guy, but how could he possibly eat all that?

"Wow," Jenny said. "That's some dinner."

"You'd be surprised what a rancher eats." Adam tucked two bottles of water under his arm.

Jenny shook her head. "I'll bet you never gain weight, either." Whereas she packed on the pounds just by thinking about the sweets she loved.

"You don't need to watch your weight," Adam said. "You're perfect the way you are."

If he only knew how flawed she was. Inside and out. "Clothes hide a multitude of sins," she replied.

"I'm not buying that, Jenny. We're coming back later for dessert."

THE ENTRY AREA off the assembly hall was deserted, just as Adam had hoped. He didn't want any sly looks or gossip about him and Jenny. Rain pounded the front exit and the roof, loud, angry slashes in the night.

"It's been pouring for hours," Jenny said. "How much longer will it last?"

"I've seen storms that go on all night. If that happens, we may be in for some flooding." Good thing the more experienced hands on his crew were capable of dealing with that.

Her eyes rounded. "Is that because the ground is so dry?"

"That, and the rivers overflowing their banks."

"Will a flood hurt your cattle or the ranch?"

"If we don't keep an eye out, it can do a fair amount of damage."

She looked worried. "Maybe you should leave now and check on your property."

Adam probably should, but he was strangely reluctant to leave Jenny just yet. "Not until I eat and you and I finish talking. If there's a problem, my foreman, Colin, will call."

"There's nowhere to sit out here," Jenny said. "I guess we could eat on the floor."

"And get that pretty dress dirty?" He shook his head. "I know just the place for us. Come with me."

Adam led her around the corner and down another hall. He stopped in front of a closed door. "As I recall, this room is unlocked. Mind holding my plate?"

He turned the knob and opened the door. Before entering, he flipped on the fluorescent lights overhead, revealing a tidy office equipped with a desk, a chair and an old, blue couch.

"This must be someone's office," Jenny said. "Or was. It looks empty now. Smells stuffy, too. Let's leave the door open."

"Sure. I've sure never seen anyone in here, and I've been using this room since eighth grade."

"Using it?" Jenny sat down on the couch. Wasting no time, she forked her salad.

Adam joined her. The couch was on the small side, but wide enough that he could sit without touching her. Otherwise he'd have sat in the office chair. Less temptation that way.

"At high-school dances, I used to sneak in here with girls," he said after devouring a chicken leg. "To fool around."

About to stab another forkful of salad, Jenny paused and shot him an incredulous look.

"Why not?" He shrugged. "This is a comfy couch. As you can see, the blinds work great, keeping things nice and private. And when the lights are out and you don't see the desk or the bare walls, it can feel pretty darned romantic."

Jenny rolled her eyes, then returned to her food.

They were both quiet for a while, eating and listening to the rain pummel the window.

"Don't tell me you never snuck off someplace to fool around with some teenage boy," Adam said when he came up for air.

"I never did. I didn't date until college."

"The guys you went to school with must've been blind."

"Well, thank you. One or two asked me out, but nothing ever came of it."

"What, your parents were extra strict?"

Jenny shook her head. "My mother had died by then, and I just… My sister and I spent a lot of time at home with Dad."

"Aw, that's sweet," Adam said. "He missed your mom, huh?"

The shadows he'd glimpsed before darkened her eyes. "Something like that."

Now he understood the cause of her pain—the death of both parents. She must've been close to them. Adam knew exactly how that felt. At least his parents had seen him married. Though neither had lived long enough to know about Abby. Or the rest.

Jenny hadn't been so lucky. When they finished eating, he stacked her empty plate on top of his, then reached over and placed both on the desk. "How old were you when your mom passed?"

"Seven." She fiddled with the cap of her water bottle. "So tell me, on which days of the week are Abby's two appointments?" she asked brightly.

Okay by him if she wanted to change the subject. "Tuesdays and Fridays after school."

"I'll take Fridays," she said.

"If you're sure. It's a long drive. I'll reimburse you for the gas."

"I offered because I want to help, Adam. I don't want your money."

No matter what she said, he hated the thought of being indebted to her. He'd definitely figure out a way to pay her back. "Thanks," he said. "I really appreciate this. Ready for dessert?" He offered her a hand up.

"I'll be sorry tomorrow, but yes."

She grasped his hand long enough to stand.

Adam didn't want to let go, but she wasn't his.

He was about to scoop the plates off the desk, when the lights flickered. An instant later, they went out.

Leaving him and Jenny in utter blackness.

Chapter Nine

Jenny squeezed her eyes shut, then opened them, hoping her vision adjusted to the sudden absence of light. She still couldn't see a thing. "What happened?" she asked, her voice floating eerily in the darkness.

"Storm must have caused an outage."

Not being able to see was disconcerting, and she reached out her arms. One hand bumped Adam's chest. Warm, solid, comforting.

He covered her hand with his, and she felt the steady thud of his heart. Longing swept through her. For what, she wasn't sure. She only knew she wanted to be in his arms. "Adam," she murmured.

"What, Jenny?"

His breath whispered across her cheek. He was going to kiss her. Aching for him, she closed her eyes.

Nothing happened.

"I want very much to kiss you," he said, as if able to see the questioning expression on her face. "But I promised I wouldn't."

He removed her hand from his chest, and she heard the soft rustle of his slacks as he stepped back, felt cool air where his warmth had been.

She was both relieved and disappointed. She also felt safe. This was a man she could trust.

"Thank you, Adam."

"For what?"

"Keeping your word."

"A man who doesn't isn't worth much."

It was just like him to say such a thing. Jenny smiled. "What're we supposed to do now?"

"Wait till someone makes their way to the boiler room and fires up the generator. We may as well sit back down."

"Okay, but how do we find the sofa?"

"It's behind us. Turn around." She felt his hands on her shoulders, gently pushing her forward. "Walk."

He sounded harsh, impatient. Jenny had no idea why.

Suddenly her shins bumped the sofa. "Here it is. Thanks, Adam."

His hands fell away, and they took a seat. Jenny didn't feel any warmth from his body, and guessed he was at the other end of the sofa, as far away as he could get.

Which was probably smart, because sitting beside him wrapped in darkness felt all too cozy and every bit as romantic as he'd said. Not exactly the right atmosphere for two people who'd agreed not to kiss each other. No wonder he'd brought girls here in high school!

Jenny settled into her corner of the sofa and wrapped her arms around her waist. "Speaking of generators," she said. "Earlier this evening Silas happened to mention that I have one in the shed behind the cottage."

"Around here, that's a given. Sometime this winter, you'll likely need it."

"I didn't know that until tonight. I've never seen a generator, and I have no idea how to operate one."

"It's not hard. I'll stop by next weekend and show you everything you need to know."

"Can you spare the time?"

"Hey, you're going to spend your valuable time driving my

kid to Red Deer and back. Showing you how to run the generator won't take long. There's one at the school, too. You'll also want to know about that one."

"So I should keep extra gas around for both?"

"Definitely."

They were both silent for a few seconds.

"It's strange, sitting here with you but not being able to see your face," Jenny said.

"Kind of like lying in bed together at night, talking the day over just before going to sleep."

Coming from Adam, the comment seemed revealing and personal, even more intimate than sex.

Her cheeks burned. How was she supposed to respond?

"I'm teasing you," Adam said. "But this does feel like that. Must be a combination of the dark, the quiet and the rain."

Jenny had always wanted to share her day with Rob just before they fell asleep, when the lights were out dark and the condo was quiet. Early on he'd let her know that for him, beds were good for two things only: sex and sleep. Most of their conversations had taken place over dinner.

She envied Adam and Simone those moments. Did he still miss them? Of course, he did. He'd loved her deeply.

"Mind if I ask you something?" Adam said.

"That all depends on if you're going to tease me or not." She smiled in the dark.

"No teasing. I'm serious."

"Okay. Go on."

"Which do you think is harder—never getting to meet your mother at all, or losing her when you're seven?"

The question was so laced with pain, Jenny winced. "I have no idea, Adam. You're wondering about Abby, huh?"

"Yeah."

She heard him scrub the back of his neck, and sensed his need to talk.

"Tell me what you're thinking."

"Maybe if she'd known Simone at least for a little while, she'd be talking today. Instead, she got stuck with me."

Jenny's heart broke for the good man beside her who'd been hurt so badly and loved his daughter so much. "Oh, Adam. It's not your fault she can't talk."

"You don't know that."

"No, but I'm pretty sure. There are lots of children who've never known their mother and have no problems speaking. And trust me, sometimes knowing your mother isn't such a great thing."

Dear God, she hadn't meant to admit that. She felt Adam startle.

"Say, what?"

Suddenly Jenny was glad the power was out, that Adam couldn't see her. She didn't think she could hide her distress or the shame for her mother's behavior that still burned inside her.

She forced a cheerful tone. "Never mind. Should we try to find our way back to the auditorium?"

"You don't say something like that and change the subject. Did your mom hurt you, Jenny?"

Adam's voice was dangerously quiet.

"Please, Adam. I can't talk about it. I can't."

"She *did* hurt you." He swore.

Just then the lights flashed on, flooding the room in harsh light. Saving her from replying.

Jenny blinked in the sudden brightness, jumped up and fled.

THE REST OF SATURDAY night, Sunday and Monday passed in a blur. Between removing dams from the overflowing river so that it didn't flood into the neighboring fields and moving the cattle out of harm's way, it'd been a hell of a long few days. Worth the effort, though, as the flood damage had been minimal, with only a few pastures affected. Early this morning the rain had stopped, the river receded, and things were back to normal.

Dinner was over. Bone-weary and sleep-deprived, Adam wanted nothing more than to relax for a while, then fall into bed and sleep like the dead. First he needed to put Abby to bed for the night.

His daughter had no problem changing into her nightgown or brushing her teeth. But she dragged her feet about actually climbing into bed, just as he had at her age.

"Tomorrow's another school day. You need your rest," he said, sounding just like his father, who'd tucked him in, no matter what ranching disaster awaited him. A busy man's way of bonding with his kid.

Had Jenny's father done the same when she was Abby's age, or had that job belonged to her abusive mother?

Jenny was abused. Adam shook his head and blew out a breath, and Abby shot him a curious look. Now was not the time for dark thoughts.

Forcing a lightheartedness he didn't feel, Adam ruffled his daughter's hair. "Pick out a book you want, and I'll read to you."

Abby nodded and, clutching Brianna, chose one of her favorites, *Corduroy,* about a toy bear in search of a friend.

No doubt she related to Corduroy. With all his heart, Adam hoped Abby made friends at school. Even one was good. He hoped his daughter learned to talk, hoped that someday she and her friend would sit up here, laughing and sharing little-girl secrets.

About halfway through the story, Abby's eyelids drifted shut.

"Sleep tight, ladybug."

Already in dreamland, she didn't object to the nickname.

Adam tucked the covers under her chin, then kissed her forehead. She smelled like toothpaste and little girl.

He turned on the Minnie Mouse night-light and left the door open a crack. Then he headed downstairs for some R & R. His first chance to relax in days.

Drew had the same idea. He was sprawled in the La-Z-Boy chair in the family room, nursing a beer, munching popcorn and watching *Monday Night Football*. By himself. Most evenings, he and Megan were glued at the hip.

"Where's your better half?" Adam asked. "I wanted to thank her in advance for agreeing to drive Abby to Red Deer tomorrow."

"You already did, but I'll let her know. She turned in early."

"Wow, that's not like her. She's usually a powerhouse."

"She worked her ass off the past two days, just like we did. I'm beat, too. Soon as this game ends, I'll be joining her. It's almost halftime. Grab yourself a beer and sit down. And, hey, as long as you're in the kitchen, you may as well bring me another."

"Only if you share that popcorn."

"Deal."

When Adam returned from the kitchen and plopped into an armchair, a halftime commercial filled the TV screen.

Drew muted the sound, then handed over the popcorn. "It's been so hectic around here, we never did get the chance to talk about that party the other night. Great spread, huh? Good band, too."

Adam had enjoyed himself—until he found out about Jenny's mother. But that wasn't likely something she'd want him to broadcast. He shrugged, then slugged back some beer. "That power outage was no fun."

Jenny's past aside, sitting in the dark with her and not

touching or kissing her had been torture. He hadn't felt such a connection to a woman in a long time.

"You sure enjoyed yourself on the dance floor. Good to see you out there after all these years."

Adam had been waiting for this. He eyed his brother. "What are you getting at?"

"You like Jenny Wyler."

Adam glared at him. "Of course, I like her. She's my daughter's teacher."

"There's more to it than that. I saw you with her. You *like* like her."

He supposed there was no use denying the truth. Not bothering with a reply, Adam shoved a handful of popcorn into his mouth.

Drew took a pull of his beer. "Gonna do anything about it?"

"Nope. She's recently out of a relationship, and that's fine by me. I have enough on my plate. Looks like the game's back on. Turn on the sound."

Adam watched the game without really seeing it. His mind was on Jenny.

And her mother. Hurting her own little girl. He still couldn't get his head around that.

He and Drew had grown up knowing that no matter what, their parents loved them. Sure, Mom or Dad might yell or ground them when they deserved it, but they never laid a hand on them, which Adam had been lucky enough to take for granted. It was the same for Abby.

Jenny hadn't been so lucky, and he wished he could go back in time and do something to protect her and keep her safe. Why hadn't her father stepped in?

Adam figured he'd never know the answer to that. For sure he didn't intend to ask Jenny. As upset as she'd been about her own comments the other night, additional questions would only rattle her more.

When one team called a time-out, Drew glanced at Adam. "Good to have you back, big brother."

What the hell did that mean? Adam frowned. "I haven't gone anywhere."

"I'm not talking physically. This is the first time you shared anything personal with me since Abby was born."

Enough with the warm fuzzies. Adam yawned and stood. "This game's a rout. There's no point watching the end. I'm turning in."

Chapter Ten

By the time Jenny turned from the highway onto the long concrete drive of Dawson Ranch early Friday evening, dusk was sliding into darkness. No doubt about it, the days were growing shorter.

Wanting to check on Abby, she glanced in the rearview mirror. Somewhere between Red Deer and Saddlers Prairie, the little girl had fallen asleep. Jenny didn't blame her. Between school and the two appointments with Carla Jenson, Abby had had a long week.

She wasn't the only one. Jenny certainly was ready for the weekend. Designing a weekly lesson plan for one grade took time enough, but eight different lesson plans? Teaching each of those plans without distracting the students in the other grades remained a continual challenge—even when she lowered her voice and worked with her students one on one. Would she ever get used to the demands of teaching in a one-room school?

"It's only been three weeks," she reminded herself out loud. Eventually she'd figure the timing and juggling act out, just as she had when teaching one grade.

As she wound slowly up the drive, she noted the porch that wrapped around the two-story house. On the main floor the curtains were pulled across the shutter-framed windows.

Still, soft light shone through, giving the house a cheerful and inviting air.

The perfect home for a normal, everyday family. The kind with healthy, loving parents, and children whose only problems were a skinned knee or getting a low grade on a test.

Growing up, Jenny had fantasized about just such a home countless times. Her fantasy had been Adam's boyhood reality. How she envied him his carefree childhood, though his life as an adult hadn't been so easy.

He was probably inside now.

After the party Saturday night she preferred to avoid him, especially his questions about her mother. Answers she wasn't about to supply. She'd come to Saddlers Prairie to escape the past, not share it.

She slowed the car to a near crawl and decided she'd drop Abby off and leave, a quick in and out. Halfway between the house and a large barn, the driveway widened substantially. Jenny rolled past the barn, Adam's truck and several Jeeps. Near the front door, she stopped. Motion-detector lights flashed on.

"Time to wake up, sleepyhead," she told Abby. "You're home."

After the little girl opened her eyes and stretched, Jenny exited the car. She opened the back door and waited for Abby to unbuckle her seat belt. Wind whipped around her, pushing her lightweight wool slacks against the backs of her legs. Autumn on the Montana prairie was beautiful, but definitely wasn't for sissies.

"Better zip your jacket," Jenny said.

She was removing the booster seat to drop it on the porch before delivering Abby and making a quick getaway, when the front door opened. Not at all ready to face Adam, Jenny forced her lips into a smile.

But instead of Adam, Mrs. Ames bustled out, wiping her

hands on her apron. Jenny was hugely relieved to not see Adam coming toward her. Yet she couldn't help wondering where he was.

"Hello, Abby," the housekeeper sang, gently touching the little girl's head. "It's good to see you again, Jenny. Welcome to Dawson Ranch."

Abby yawned and leaned into the housekeeper.

"I'm afraid she fell asleep in the car." Jenny handed over the booster seat. "She may be up late tonight. Tell Adam I'm sorry."

"He'll be happy about that. He's still out with Drew—they rode out a while ago to take care of a couple of problem heifers. He doesn't expect to be back until later. This way he'll be able to tuck her in."

Then Jenny *wouldn't* see him. For the first time since turning into the driveway, she pulled in a full breath.

"Thanks so much for taking Abby to Red Deer and bringing her home," Mrs. Ames said. "You can't see much in the dark, but the barn is well-lit. There's enough time for Megan to give you that five-cent tour while I finish up with dinner, if you like. You'll stay, of course."

Jenny wanted to see the ranch, but she wasn't so sure about dinner. Somehow eating with the family seemed too personal, even with Adam away. Besides, staying would increase her chances of running into him.

She shook her head. "I really can't. Maybe some other time?"

"You're not having dinner with us?" Mrs. Ames looked disappointed.

"Um." *Make something up, Jenny.* "I didn't know I was invited." As excuses went, that one was pretty lame.

"Of course you are. After your long drive, I know you must be famished. I'll bet you are, too, Abby. I usually don't eat with the family, but I will tonight. I was so looking forward to a just-us-girls dinner."

Abby tugged on Jenny's sleeve, drawing her attention downward.

The little girl angled her chin and widened her eyes, clearly expressing herself despite her inability to speak. She, too, wanted Jenny to stay.

Disappointing this special child was the last thing Jenny wanted. This was simply a dinner invitation for the teacher. Adam was out, so what could it hurt? She smiled at Abby. "I'd love to have dinner with you."

"I'VE NEVER BEEN IN A BARN," Jenny said, taking in the large space and high ceilings. "It smells good. Pungent yet sweet."

"It should—I just mucked out the stinky stuff." Megan's mouth quirked. She and Jenny were alone, as Abby had gone inside with Mrs. Ames to use the bathroom and change clothes. "This is one of Abby's favorite places to hang out. She likes the horses. That's what you smell—horses and hay."

Jenny knew nothing about caring for the big animals, or cattle, either, for that matter.

"The other barn smells different," Megan went on. "Or it will when the men finish with the reconstruction, sometime next week, if all goes well."

"There's *another* barn? This one is so huge."

"We're a pretty big ranch," Megan said. "The other one sits on property we recently annexed. It was a real dump, so we tore it down and started over, but it's coming along. Adam and Drew were taking turns supervising until they hired someone to do the job. A good thing, too, since they're putting in twelve-to-fourteen-hour days right now."

Adam hadn't been kidding about working hard. "And I thought my days were long," she murmured.

"We're so grateful to you for driving Abby to Red Deer

once a week. There's just too much for me to do around here to take her to both appointments." Even though Abby was inside, Megan lowered her voice. "Do you really think that speech therapist can help her?"

"Absolutely. Carla Jenson believes without a doubt that she can teach Abby to talk. And so do I. I'm working hard on doing my part at school."

"Here at the ranch, too. We all take our turns."

"That's great."

"Then why are you frowning?" Megan asked. "Should we *not* be helping her?"

"Of course you should. It's just…" Unsure about discussing Abby with Megan instead of Adam, Jenny hesitated. But this was Adam's sister-in-law, Abby's aunt. She already knew everything about the little girl, and was obviously interested in her welfare. Jenny saw no reason to hold back her concerns. "I just wish Abby would let down her guard around the other kids," she confided.

From out of nowhere, a black cat darted toward the barn door. To Jenny's surprise, Abby suddenly appeared, as well, and followed the cat. Jenny hadn't realized she was there. How much had she heard?

By Megan's worried look, she was also concerned.

The barn filled with plaintive meows as the cat rubbed against Abby's legs. With a defiant look at Jenny, the little girl scooped up the animal and cuddled her like a doll.

She'd definitely heard that last part.

Megan cleared her throat. "Meet Jezebel. She and Abby are longtime friends."

Abby's closemouthed smile all but screamed, *See? I can let down my guard if I want to.*

Figuring she'd better explain her comment, Jenny pulled in a breath. "You're lucky to have such a special animal friend,

Abby. She must really trust you. You trust her, too, don't you?"

The little girl dipped her head as she often did at school. By now, Jenny knew her well enough, and realized that even though she didn't respond, she *was* listening.

"People, including children, make good friends, too," Jenny went on. "That's what I want for you, Abby, and that's what I meant about letting down your guard." She glanced at Megan, who raised her eyebrows, then continued, "But you don't have to do that, ever, unless you want to. Okay?"

At last Abby looked at Jenny and gave a reluctant nod. Purring loudly, Jezebel jumped down and flounced off.

"I need a hug," Jenny said, opening her arms. "How about you?"

The little girl came willingly. Jenny held her tight. Abby hung on, her arms wrapped sweetly around Jenny's neck. Jenny's heart overflowed. When she finally let Abby go, she knew that they were once again on good terms.

Megan wore a tender smile. "It must be almost time to eat. Let's take Miss Wyler inside, Abby, and show her around."

As if understanding the conversation, the cat followed them up the porch steps and through the back door. They passed through a mudroom, where coats hung on hooks, and boots and shoes were paired neatly under a bench along the wall.

Abby opened the door to the kitchen. Delicious smells greeted Jenny, making her glad she'd accepted the dinner invitation.

Standing over a steaming pot on the stove, Mrs. Ames smiled. "Perfect timing—dinner's almost ready. Come and help me, Abby and Megan. You two wash up at the kitchen sink, but let's send our guest to the powder room. Head down the hall and past the living room, first door on your right.

Hope you don't mind if we eat in here instead of the dining room, Jenny."

Jenny glanced around the sparkling kitchen, with its tile counters and family-size, round oak table in the center of the room. "Not at all."

She wandered down the hall, toward the living room.

The spacious room was every bit as welcoming as she'd imagined. Thick, braided rugs covered sections of the gleaming wood floors. The pale yellow walls were decorated with framed oils and watercolors, and the furniture scattered through the room looked comforting and inviting. She could picture the Dawsons relaxing in here.

The powder room was a whole different place—pale blue wallpaper dotted with tiny, colorful flowers, and lacy curtains across the window. A surprisingly feminine room.

"That bathroom wasn't what I expected," Jenny commented when she returned to the kitchen.

Mrs. Ames laughed. "Everybody says that. Mrs. Dawson Senior decorated it. She said that with a house full of males, she needed something frilly. Please, sit down."

Steaming platters filled the lazy Susan in the middle of the table.

"May I sit next to you, Abby?" Jenny asked.

The little girl beamed and showed Jenny her seat.

"In that case, you can help her dish up her food," Mrs. Ames said.

"Of course. Do you live on the ranch, Mrs. Ames?" Jenny asked as she spooned pot roast onto Abby's plate and her own.

The housekeeper nodded. "I have my own apartment at the back of the house. I get weekends and holidays off. Early tomorrow I'm off to visit my sister in Sidney. That's about ninety miles west of here."

"Mrs. Ames has been here since Adam and Drew were babies," Megan added.

"So Adam told me."

Both Mrs. Ames and Megan shot her curious looks.

"I'm surprised he told you that," Megan said. "He doesn't usually talk about anything personal."

"He mentioned it at the dance the other night."

"Isn't that interesting." Suddenly Megan looked like the proverbial cat who ate the canary.

Jenny had no idea why as there was nothing going on between her and Adam. Still, she blushed. "Would you like gravy on your mashed potatoes?" she asked Abby.

The little girl shook her head.

"I'll bet you don't know how I came to live here," Mrs. Ames said. "My Jimmy was foreman for Graham Dawson— Adam and Drew's daddy. When Jimmy died, the family invited me to stay on as their housekeeper."

"She has all the goods on Adam and Drew." Megan winked.

Which Adam had also mentioned. Not wanting any more knowing looks, Jenny kept that to herself.

"They were raised right, too. Today they're as honest and straightforward as their father and grandfather," Mrs. Ames said.

With everyone served, they dug in. This was no ordinary pot roast. Wonderful flavors exploded in Jenny's mouth. The mashed potatoes and green beans were every bit as delicious.

"This is the best food I've ever eaten," she raved.

Mrs. Ames beamed. "It's an old Dawson family recipe. I'm sure your family has a few that your mother cooks for you."

If Jenny's mother had ever cooked, she didn't remember. "I wouldn't know. She died when I was a little girl."

"I'm sorry," Mrs. Ames said, putting down her fork.

"Gosh, I had no idea." Megan bit her lip. "That's rough."

Jenny was relieved that Adam hadn't said anything to either woman. While she didn't mind their knowing, she didn't want to deal with the questions. "It was a long time ago," she said.

Abby's somber and knowing expression made her look worlds older. Jenny hurt for the little girl who'd lost so much.

She recalled Adam's question the other night. Was it better to know your mother for a little while than never at all? For Abby, knowing her mother probably would've been better.

Sometimes life was so unfair.

"We're alike that way, Abby," Jenny said. "Neither of us has a mother."

The sympathetic look on the sweet little face warmed Jenny. Abby reached for her hand, and Jenny's heart melted into a big puddle of love.

MOST WEEKEND MORNINGS, Adam did his and Drew's chores, so that his brother and Megan could sleep in. By their sleepy, satisfied smiles when they wandered into the kitchen around lunchtime Sunday, they'd enjoyed a lot more than a long night's rest.

That did squat for Adam's foul mood. Lately, nothing did.

He greeted them, then tromped outside. Wanting a woman he could never have was no damn fun. He hadn't even seen or spoken to Jenny in over a week, not since the night of the dance when she'd bolted out of the community center office.

Despite not seeing her, though, he sure had been thinking of her. He wanted to find out about her childhood, wanted answers to questions he had no right to ask. More than that, he wanted to see Jenny and make sure she was okay. That's what he told himself, but he knew that wasn't the whole reason.

The simple truth was, he wanted to see her. Yet at the same time, he didn't. What was the point when he'd promised to keep his hands to himself?

Regardless, in less than an hour, he'd knock at her door.

Today was a normal end-of-September day, windless and sunny. A welcome reprieve from the cold wind and nasty rain they'd been having. With any luck the good weather would hold another week or so until they finished the vaccinating and weaning.

In the barn, Adam collected the rust remover, tools and paint from various shelves. He set them in the truck, along with a couple of full cans of gas.

Suddenly, the back door opened, and Drew and Megan wandered onto the porch.

"Going someplace?" Drew called out.

Adam shaded his eyes against the sun. "I promised to help Jenny with her generator."

"Generator? Is that what you're calling it?" Drew snickered.

"Drew!" Laughing, Megan jabbed him with her elbow.

Drew nuzzled her neck, and her mirthful expression faded into something hot and suggestive.

Another minute and they'd be all over each other. Adam rolled his eyes. "Didn't you two get enough of that this morning?"

Without a trace of embarrassment, Drew flung his arm around Megan. "I'll never get enough of my wife," he drawled.

"Could you keep your pants zipped till I get back? I need you to keep an eye on Abby." Adam gestured at the opposite side of the house. "She's on the tree swing."

Drew and Megan exchanged needy looks. "When exactly will that be?" Drew asked.

Not about to spend any more time with Jenny than necessary, Adam shrugged. "However long it takes."

After striding to the side yard to tell his daughter goodbye, he slid into the truck and headed out.

The drive took all of ten minutes. On the way there, Adam calculated how much time he needed. Running a generator wasn't too complicated. Throw in cleaning and paint touch-ups, and he'd be home again in about two hours.

Away from temptation.

Once he arrived, he parked the truck next to Jenny's car. His heart thudded loudly as he wiped his feet on the welcome mat and knocked on her front door. Seconds later she opened it.

She looked surprised to see him, and by her lack of a smile, not exactly thrilled.

"Adam." She brushed the hair from her face and tugged her sweatshirt over her hips. Gestures he now understood meant she was flustered.

His hungry eyes drank her in. Just the sight of her messed with his hormones. He was in trouble here. They were already on shaky ground, so he'd best watch himself so he didn't try to kiss her again.

"What are you doing here?" Jenny asked.

"We talked about this last Saturday night. I said I'd be over this weekend, and show you how to run the generator here and the one at school."

"I know, but…I just didn't… Never mind. Come in."

Given his ever-increasing attraction to Jenny, the little house didn't have near enough space for the two of them. Adam stayed put. "Why don't I just do a quick walk around outside and find the hookup. It's probably out back. Then I'll grab that generator from the shed and set it up."

"Wait—I'll come with you."

The last thing he needed was Jenny shadowing him. "That's okay. You wait here," he said, leaving.

She shook her head and caught up to him. "I want to learn how to do everything, and that includes locating the hookup and bringing the generator out of the shed."

"Suit yourself." Adam found what he was looking for near the kitchen window. "This is the box where the generator connects to the house."

"Are you angry with me, Adam?"

He was more mad at himself for not corralling his feelings. He was also bothered by other things he preferred to keep to himself. The words slipped out anyway. "Friday night, you had dinner with Megan, Abby and Mrs. Ames." He turned toward the shed.

"Yes, I did," Jenny said, scrambling to keep up. "Is that a problem?"

"It is when no one told me until the next day."

Jenny hadn't felt comfortable with him at the dance and had run away from him. Yet she'd been perfectly happy to sit down at his family kitchen table, talking about God knew what with Megan and Mrs. Ames. Adam had no idea what they'd discussed. Megan sure hadn't shared much. And with Mrs. Ames gone, he couldn't ask her, and wouldn't anyway. As for Abby, she couldn't exactly tell him anything.

"I hadn't planned on staying, only to drop Abby off and leave. It was spur of the moment." She sighed. "You and Drew were doing something with your cattle, and I guess Megan and Mrs. Ames wanted the company. Plus Abby really wanted me to stay. And she's hard to turn down."

Adam sure knew that, and was pleased that Jenny was so enamored of his little girl.

"Thanks for driving Abby to her appointment," he said grudgingly.

"You're welcome. I enjoyed finally meeting Carla Jenson in person."

"Is that what you talked about at dinner?"

Jenny shook her head. "We mostly chatted about food and the ranch. Before dinner, Megan showed me around a little, but it was too dark to see much. I'm awed by what I *did* see, though. Actually, by your entire operation. You have a lot to be proud of."

Adam *was* proud. "My grandfather started with a modest ranch of four hundred acres and one-hundred-seventy cattle. My father quadrupled that, and Drew and I are following suit. Megan probably told you all that."

"Actually, she explained more about the horses in the barn. I never realized how much work goes into caring for them." As they reached the shed, Jenny gave him a sideways glance. "You really didn't miss anything, Adam."

He followed her in, ducking his head as he stepped through the low door.

Aside from the generator, the musty little shack was filled with the usual lawn mower, hose and gardening tools. He couldn't stand up straight without bumping his head on the ceiling, and there was barely enough room for him to turn around, let alone put much space between him and Jenny.

She was close enough to see for him to note the gold flecks in her eyes and smell her flowery shampoo. Her mouth pursed as it sometimes did, looking somewhere between a sexy pout and a teacherly scolding.

She was killing him, and she didn't even know it. He had to get her out of here.

He stalked toward the generator, which was seated on a wheeled carrier. "Let me drag this thing outside. You carry this," he said, thrusting its canvas cover at her.

"You don't have to be rude about it."

Hugging the tarp, Jenny stepped outside.

Adam pulled the generator forward. The thing weighed more than it looked, and he grunted as he lifted it out of the shed.

Jenny's eyes were huge.

"What?" he barked.

"Nothing. Just…you're really strong."

He saw admiration in her eyes, and liked it. He hauled the generator behind the house and set it near the kitchen window.

"This is how you attach it." He showed Jenny where to add gas, how to set the choke and what to do if she flooded the motor.

She caught on even faster than he'd figured, but then she was really smart.

"I think I should try it now to make sure I can do it." She glanced up at him, her lips slightly parted.

The urge to kiss her hit him hard. Silently cursing, Adam stepped back. "Just go through the motions like I did."

She copied him exactly.

"Good job," he said. "Now let's put the tarp on, and then we'll head for school." As soon as he checked the generator there and showed her how to start it, he'd drop her back here and leave. It couldn't be soon enough.

Chapter Eleven

With his gaze fixed straight ahead, his jaw set and both hands gripping the wheel, Adam was more tense than Jenny had ever seen him. He was in an awful mood. All because he'd stopped by to help her with the generator—help she hadn't even asked for.

At this point, she wasn't sure how she felt about Adam. Watching him wrestle the heavy piece of equipment from the shed, his biceps bunching, T-shirt stretching across his broad back... Jenny stifled a sigh. He was by far the strongest, physically fit man she'd ever known. But his mood shifts were confusing. When he wasn't abrupt and aggravated with her, she'd catch him looking at her, his blue eyes hooded and hungry. In those moments, her body had responded as if he'd caressed her, and she wanted him as she'd never desired a man. Five seconds later, he was snapping at her.

Talk about your mixed messages.

Then again, what did it matter what he thought of her when getting involved with Adam Dawson was not an option?

He didn't so much as glance at her until he pulled into the school driveway. His brows drew together in a scowl.

Jenny let out an irritated sigh. "What's wrong now, Adam?"

"I don't know what you mean." Jaw set, he rolled to a stop.

Refusing to leave the truck until they cleared the air, Jenny flipped the power locks on her side of the truck.

Adam could've unlocked them, but didn't. "What'd you do that for?"

"You're so tense, you're making *me* tense. You're put out with me, and not because you volunteered to help with the generators. What's going on?"

"Let it be, will you?"

Jenny crossed her arms and shook her head.

"Brother, you're stubborn." He gave her a wary look. "You'll get mad."

"I'm already halfway there because of your bad mood." She raised her eyebrows. "Talk to me, Adam."

He scrubbed his hand over his face, then exhaled. "All right, all right. It's about the night of the dance, when you ran away."

"I did no such thing! It was late, and I needed to go home. And so did you, remember? The rain and possible flooding?"

"You never even said goodbye. There's more to your behavior than wanting to get home. A lot more, and we both know it."

Jenny rolled her eyes. Why hadn't she seen this coming? Because until this moment, the subject hadn't come up, and she'd assumed Adam had let it go. *Wrong.*

Her heart stuttered in her chest, and her hands went ice-cold, but she managed to hide her mounting panic under a calm facade. "It was a long time ago—hardly worth talking about," she replied in what she thought was a quite reasonable tone. "Besides, didn't we both agree that our pasts should stay in the past?"

"What'd I tell you—you're all riled up."

Apparently she *hadn't* sounded so reasonable. What could she say to that?

"I'm right there with you," Adam went on. "How could a mother hurt her own daughter?"

Jenny wasn't about to explain. But Adam clearly expected a reply, and she doubted he'd drop the matter until she answered. "She didn't do it on purpose," she said.

"Make all the excuses you want, Jenny. The end result is still the same. Your mother abused you."

He was wrong. The deep hurt had come from her mother's mental illness, her inability to show love for Jenny, Becca or their father, and the ensuing shame that hovered over the family like a dark cloud, not physical abuse. April Wyler had never raised a hand to her.

None of which Adam would ever know.

"That subject is not open for discussion," Jenny said. "Unless you want to first tell me why you blame yourself for Abby's speech problems?"

That shut him up.

"Just show me how to work the school generator, okay?" Jenny unlocked the doors and slid out of the truck. "Then we can both go home."

SHADING HER EYES FROM the slanting afternoon sun, Jenny frowned at the monstrosity behind the school. Adam had just pulled the tarp off the generator. They were both trying hard to get along.

"I thought that was some obsolete piece of equipment no one had bothered to remove," she said.

"Nope, this is your generator. The same one that was here when I was in school."

"Then it's been around awhile. You'd think the school district would replace it with a newer model."

"Hey, it still works great, and they don't exactly have the funds to spare."

"What's the brown stuff all over it?"

Adam looked at her as if she'd just arrived from another planet. "It's called rust."

"I know what rust is, but I've never seen so much of it. No wonder the school put a tarp over this thing. It's a big eyesore."

He muttered something about big-city women. "The tarp protects the generator from the weather, but sometimes moisture creeps in anyway. With a good cleaning and a fresh coat of paint, it'll look good as new."

Jenny could think of better ways to spend the rest of her day. She needed to clean the house and fine-tune the lesson plans for Abby to incorporate some of the things she'd learned from Carla Jenson. But if she wanted to make sure the school always had power, maintenance on the generator was just as important.

"Okay," she said. "How exactly do I clean this thing?"

"Silas is your landlord. He ought to take care of this for you. But since I'm here and I brought the rust remover and cleaning supplies with me, I'll do it. It'll go faster if I work by myself."

With the mulish look on his face, she knew better than to try to talk him out of the job. "If that's what you want. I'll paint it later. I assume Silas has the right kind of paint—or maybe Spenser's?"

"I'm sure they both do, but I brought my own. I'll do the painting."

"Are you sure you have time?" she said.

He squinted in the sunlight as if trying to assess her sincerity.

Jenny shrugged. "You said you wanted to get this over with."

"I do, but I don't mind." He headed for the truck.

Jenny watched him go, admiring his easy, long-limbed gait. How could loose, faded jeans look so good on a man?

In seconds, he was back with the supplies. He set them beside the generator, then settled his hands low on his hips. "Isn't there something you could do inside while I take care of this?"

She'd have been perfectly content to watch him work, but apparently he preferred his own company. She glanced over her shoulder, at the back door. "There are a few things I'd planned to do before school tomorrow. I'll just do them now."

The weather was mild enough that she left both doors open. Fresh air flooded the room, and she could hear the grate of steel wool against the metal sides of the generator as Adam started to work.

She couldn't help wondering whether scrubbing away at the rust caused Adam's muscles to bunch. Or what they felt like when they contracted like that.

She didn't dare peek for fear he'd catch her drooling.

"Get over him, Jenny," she muttered. "You are not interested."

Some fifty minutes later, she was writing the vocabulary word for the day on the whiteboard when a shadow fell across the floor.

Adam stood on the threshold. "All done."

Maybe it was the sun shining at his back that made his eyes look so strikingly blue—a blue she could easily drown in. All she knew was that she wouldn't mind melting into his solid warmth, either. With effort she tore her gaze from his. "Wow, you *are* fast. Thanks, Adam. I don't know what I'd have done without your help."

"No problem. Like I said, I owe you."

"Will you quit saying that?"

Hands on her hips, she scrutinized him. Still standing on the threshold, he shifted his weight, scratched his chin. "Did I just sprout blue hair or something?"

"You have a black smudge on your cheek." She tapped her finger on her own face. "Right there."

Adam rubbed at the spot. "Did I get it?"

Jenny shook her head. "Come in while I get some water and a rag."

"No need. I'll take care of it when I get home," Adam said, yet he stepped inside.

In the bathroom, Jenny partially filled a basin with warm water. She carried it, a rag and a bar of soap to her desk and set them down. "Now sit."

"You don't need to do this," Adam said.

"You've been doing things for me all afternoon." She pointed at her chair.

After rolling his eyes at the ceiling and muttering, he complied.

Jenny wet and lathered the rag. Gingerly she soaped Adam's cheek. Her knuckles brushed his skin.

Adam flinched.

"Are you okay?"

"Yep." He stared straight ahead.

Jenny began to scrub, her senses alive with the man before her. He smelled of sweat and his own scent. She felt the heat from his body, sensed the masculine strength within him.

Her nerves began to hum. Lips compressed, she worked on the paint spot. Rubbing the rag over it, back and forth, around and around. Rinsing off the soap, checking the smudge, rubbing again…

"What's taking so long?" Adam said through gritted teeth.

He sounded as though he was in pain, and he'd already flinched. Jenny frowned. "Sorry, but it isn't coming off. Does it hurt?"

"It hurts, all right." He finally looked at her, his eyes bright and hot.

Her whole body tingled. She stilled. Swallowed. "Um… Maybe I shouldn't rub your skin so hard."

A strained laugh broke from his lips, and he nodded at his groin. "It's not my skin that's hard."

She glanced at the erection straining his fly, and her mouth went dry. "So—sorry."

She meant to back away, only her legs refused to move. The rag dropped from her fingers. "Adam," she said. "I—"

"Don't say a word," he growled, wiping his face on the hem of his shirt. "Just get out of my way."

The legs of the chair scraped back and he started to stand.

"Don't go." She cupped his rock-solid shoulders.

Adam circled her wrists and lifted her hands off him before pushing her away, forcing her unwilling legs to cooperate. "Are you *trying* to torture me?"

Knowing how badly he wanted her only upped her own desire. "This isn't exactly easy for me, either," she said.

His eyes burned into her, and the words tumbled out. "I know you won't go back on your word, Adam, but I'm begging you to do it anyway. If you don't kiss me now, I swear, I'll die."

THE LONGING ON JENNY'S FACE and the plea in her voice broke the last of Adam's resolve. With a groan, he tugged her onto his lap and kissed her. Hard, so she knew he wasn't kidding around.

She wrapped her arms around his neck and pressed her body close. She kissed him back, all heat and promise.

Adam urged her lips apart, slipped his tongue into the heaven of her mouth. She tasted like hungry woman, her tongue sliding over his, then darting back. Teasing, driving him wild.

He grasped her hips, pushing her against his throbbing erection.

Just as his hands slipped inside the hem of her sweatshirt, Jenny broke the kiss. They were both winded.

"This can't turn into anything, and no one can know," she said between deep breaths.

"No one." He kissed her again.

A long time later, after he knew the soft heft of her breasts, the sharp peaks of her aroused nipples and the little moaning sounds she made when she especially liked his attention, he tugged her sweatshirt down and set her off his lap.

"I've got to get going," he said. "We should head out."

Before he did something really crazy and took her right here on the teacher's desk. Now there was an intriguing thought.

Neither of them said a word on the drive back to her house. Adam pulled to a stop in her driveway, the engine idling. He reached across to open her door for her, but Jenny laid her hand on his, stopping him. She turned to him and he was lost.

They kissed again like a pair of crazed teenagers making out for the first time.

Adam couldn't get enough of her mouth. Of her.

He wanted more than kisses. A lot more, and he sensed Jenny did, too. But it was too soon.

One more long, sweet taste and they broke apart.

"I'll be in touch," Adam said.

Jenny nodded, then fluffed her hair and smoothed her sweatshirt.

This time he let her open her own door. The late afternoon air, cooler now, flooded the truck. Pausing, she glanced at him over her shoulder. "Good night, Adam."

He waited for a few seconds until she was safely inside. Then he drove away with an aching hard-on and a sappy grin on his face.

Chapter Twelve

Just over two weeks later, sleepy after another late night with Adam, Jenny stood in front of the classroom's baseboard heater before school, sipping coffee from her thermos and shivering. This would be another flawless day, and in a few hours the sun would warm the air inside and out, and then she'd be able to turn off the heat.

At the moment, though, she could almost see her breath in here. No doubt a taste of winter, which everyone in town warned could come at any time. The mid-October wind certainly felt sharper and colder, and the air no longer smelled sweet, which was very different from the weather six weeks ago. But then, over the past few weeks, a lot had changed. Specifically since she'd shamelessly begged Adam to kiss her and he'd pulled her onto his lap in this very room.

Since then, nothing had been the same between them.

No longer cold, Jenny smiled and moved to the whiteboard at the front of the room. She printed the vocabulary word of the day and today's date.

But her thoughts were on last night, when Adam had stopped by the cottage. Something he did several times a week. Always on the sly, as they agreed that no one should know they were seeing each other. Especially Abby. So that she wouldn't get hurt, neither of them wanted to involve her in any way. Hiding what they did seemed safest.

Jenny's cell phone buzzed, signaling a text message. She slipped it from her pocket. The message was from Adam. *Thinking about you and last night.*

The mere mention of their evening together and she all but melted. "You aren't the only one," she murmured.

Last night they'd come close to making love, but Jenny wasn't ready, and Adam had stopped. That didn't mean they couldn't give each other pleasure. And Adam's sensitivity to her body, to what she liked and wanted, gave her intense pleasure. Jenny had no doubt that sometime in the near future, she and Adam would become lovers.

The things he did with his mouth and his hands... Her body began to hum and stir with need, but school was about to start, and she still had things to do. She pushed the feelings away. *I enjoyed last night, too,* she texted back. *Have fun weighing those yearlings. Turning phone off now.*

She searched through a manila folder for today's math worksheets, sorting by aptitude, not grade level. Most of her students were way ahead of the norm. As soon as she finished the chore, her thoughts returned to Adam.

To her relief, he'd stopped asking about her past. In turn, she'd stopped wondering about his. By some unspoken agreement, they also ignored the future, focusing only on the here and now. No promises, no words of love. They simply enjoyed each other's company and delighted in their mutual, steadily growing passion.

Just before nine o'clock, students began to drift in. In no time, Jenny was standing before them, signaling the beginning of the school day.

"Good morning, class," she said.

"Good morning, Miss Wyler," everyone replied. Except, of course, Abby.

"First, announcements. Parent-teacher meetings are next week, which means that Tuesday through Friday, you'll get out of school at noon instead of three. This afternoon, I'll pass out the information. Please give it to your parents."

After a pause to make sure every student had paid attention, she continued, "All right, let's move on. Martin, it's your turn to take attendance."

With so few students, formal attendance-taking really wasn't necessary, but Jenny preferred to do it anyway, as a way of teaching responsibility, and for each student to acknowledge the others. They seemed to like it.

The fifth-grade boy eagerly joined her at the front of the room.

"Today we're going to try something different," Jenny said. "Will you please take attendance in reverse alphabetical order." A fun idea she'd never considered until coming to Saddlers Prairie. "Who can tell me what reverse alphabetical order is?"

Several hands shot up. Jenny nodded at Julie Eden, her lone seventh-grader. "Julie?"

"Instead of going from *A* to *Z*, you go from *Z* to *A*," the girl explained.

"Exactly. Are you willing to try that, Martin?"

The boy gave an enthusiastic nod. Jenny handed him the attendance chart and sat down at her desk.

"Since my last name is Volles, I guess I'm first. No wait, my sister is first." He glanced at Jenny, and she nodded her approval. "Suzanne Volles."

The second-grader raised her hand. "Here."

"Now me—Martin Volles. Here," he said, raising his own hand. Jenny and the other students laughed.

Martin continued through the list without a hitch. "Abby Dawson."

Abby raised her hand. Martin was about to read another name, when Abby's lips moved. "H-h-h-here."

The stunned expression on Martin's face would've been

comical, only this was a moment far too momentous for humor.

Abby had just spoken her first word.

"Would you mind repeating that?" Jenny asked.

All heads turned toward Abby and everyone caught their collective breaths.

"Here." Abby's voice rang loud in the otherwise silent room.

Jenny laid both palms over her chest and teared up. The entire class burst into spontaneous applause.

The little girl beamed more brightly than the morning sun.

Jenny could hardly wait to share the fantastic news with Adam. She'd call him during recess, she decided. It couldn't come soon enough.

ADAM, DREW AND A COUPLE of hands were weighing yearlings in the scale shed when his cell rang. Not sure he wanted to take the time to answer, he slid the thing from his pocket and checked the screen.

"Who is it, bro?" Drew asked.

"Jenny."

Calling in the middle of the school day? She wouldn't do that unless something was wrong. Panic gripped him.

Drew hooted. "Guess she got sick of waiting for you to make the firs—"

Adam silenced him with a look. He pivoted away and strode out of the shed for privacy.

"What's happened?" he said, not bothering to waste time on pleasantries.

"It's unbelievable, Adam," she said, sounding breathless. "Abby just said her first word."

Not sure he'd heard right, he frowned. "What did you say?"

"We were taking attendance. When her name was called,

she raised her hand and said 'here,' just like any other student. I asked her to repeat herself, and she did."

Adam didn't remember the rest of the conversation, except that Jenny's joy matched his, and that he'd said to let Abby know he'd pick her up after school.

He hung up and returned to the shed.

"What's with the big grin on your face?" Drew asked.

"A miracle happened this morning. Abby talked."

WANTING TO GREET HIS little girl without nosy parents and their kids watching the show, Adam timed his arrival at school for after the other kids left.

Whistling tunelessly, he entered the classroom.

Abby was waiting for him with an open, expectant face. Jenny's affection for his daughter shone in her eyes. She seemed awed and proud of Abby, the way a mother would.

For one brief moment, Adam imagined a different world, one where Jenny *was* Abby's mother.

Where had *that* come from?

Simone was Abby's mother. And she was gone.

Oblivious of his thoughts, Jenny smiled. So much warmth, passion, smarts and beauty. She took his breath away. He thought about her all the time. About making her smile. Kissing her, touching her and, once she was ready, loving her the way a man was meant to love a woman.

But his feelings stopped at lust. Neither of them wanted more.

Tearing his gaze from Jenny's, Adam grinned at his daughter. "Miss Wyler shared some exciting news with me."

Jenny nodded. "I told Abby about our phone call. We're going to have quite a parent-teacher meeting next week."

Her nurturing hand settled on his daughter's shoulder, much the way Adam's often did. Abby leaned into her teacher's warmth and shined a sublimely happy smile up at her.

Jenny's genuine fondness for Abby meant a great deal to Adam. He wanted to express his gratitude by pulling her close and kissing her senseless, but he couldn't do that just now. His private thanks and show of appreciation would have to wait until later.

"I'd like to hear the sound of your voice," he told Abby. "Will you talk for me?"

She hesitated. Chewed her lip and looked up at Jenny with such a heartfelt need for encouragement that Adam's chest hurt.

His daughter trusted her teacher. More than that, she adored her.

Adam totally understood. He was halfway there himself. The thought dumbfounded him. Hadn't he just silently stated that what he felt for Jenny was lust, nothing more?

Right now his feelings were so strong, he knew he'd lied to himself about what he really wanted.

A real relationship with Jenny Wyler. A future.

The very thought scared him witless. He must be out of his mind, letting himself care. Jenny didn't want that, and God knew what she'd do if she found out how he truly felt. She was skittish enough about anything that hinted at the past or the future.

Adam wasn't that stupid. He wasn't about to serve himself up to that kind of heartbreak. Once had been more than enough.

From now on, he was pulling back. Way back. Until he was so far away, he no longer cared.

"Go ahead, sweetheart," Jenny said with an encouraging smile. "Tell your daddy what you said to your classmates this afternoon."

Abby stood up straight, raised her little chin and spoke. "Bye."

Her voice was soft, but the word was clear and easy to understand. His daughter had finally interacted with other kids. Tears ached behind Adam's eyes, pushing to get out. He didn't even try to stop them.

With fingers that trembled, he swiped at the moisture. Jenny's eyes were watery, too. They shared a long, meaningful look. She understood and cared more than he had any right to expect her to, which only reinforced his growing feelings. He shoved them away.

"This is a big step, and I'm so proud of you," he told Abby. "I think we should celebrate tonight. How about we go out for ice cream sundaes at Barb's?"

Without a trace of hesitation, his daughter rubbed her stomach and licked her lips. Then she pointed at Jenny.

"You want Miss Wyler to come along." He eyed Jenny. "Well?"

Her sober, silent look was easy to interpret. People would see them together at the family celebration. News that was sure to spread like a wildfire, causing all manner of talk and speculation. For Abby's sake, Jenny didn't want that. Neither did Adam. Especially now.

He half hoped she'd turn down the invitation, but at the same time, he hated to see his little girl disappointed on such a special day. He gave Jenny a barely perceptible nod.

She smiled at Abby. "An ice-cream celebration with you and the rest of your family? Of course, I'll come!"

THE ONE POSITIVE OF GOING to Barb's after dinner was you missed the crowd, Adam thought as he followed his family and Jenny inside. This wouldn't be so bad—just smile, get through the evening and leave. Then he spotted Anita Eden and one of her girlfriends in the corner table. Her sly look turned his mood south in a hurry.

Jenny noticed, too—Adam knew by the quick, nervous glance she darted at him. She was with Megan, deep in some animated conversation. Drew and Abby stuck close behind the women. Adam hung back.

Donna was on duty tonight. She greeted them with her usual toothy smile. "Did you see my Anita over there? Barb and Emilio figured you'd come in tonight for ice cream, even though it isn't your birthday, Abby. We heard the good news." Donna regarded Jenny with an astute look that rivaled her daughter's. "It's good to see you, Jenny. How nice that you're joining the Dawson family celebration."

Adam could almost hear the phone lines buzz.

Since he never intended to touch Jenny again, the whole nosy bunch would soon learn that there was nothing to their talk.

He waited until Jenny slid into a booth, then gestured at Megan. "Go ahead."

"Are you sure?" Megan asked.

Less togetherness, less talk among the diners—and between him and Jenny. Adam nodded. "I'll sit at the end."

Donna pulled out her order pad. "Ice-cream sundaes all around, or does someone want one of Emilio's homemade brownies with ice cream and fudge sauce?"

Adam waited until after Jenny, Megan and Drew ordered. "Sundaes, two scoops each, with extra chocolate for Abby and me," he said. She'd probably waste half, but he wanted her to feel extra special.

"Abby, tonight your ice cream is on us. Would you like the usual extra cherry on top?"

His daughter opened her mouth as if she wanted to reply, then pressed her lips together instead.

"Come on, Abby, you can do this," Adam urged. "It's one little word. 'Yes.' Say it."

Jenny widened her eyes at him, and he realized he was riding her too hard. He forced a nonchalant expression.

Too late. His daughter ducked her head.

No talking tonight.

"It's okay, sweetie," Jenny said, rubbing Abby's back. "The *y* sound is difficult. We'll practice at school."

An explanation delivered for everyone's benefit, yet Adam sensed an underlying censure directed at him. Talking was too new, and his daughter was too shy and insecure to test a new sound in front of an audience. She needed patience and understanding.

For pushing her, he felt about two feet tall. "Give her the two cherries," he growled at Donna.

JENNY SETTLED BETWEEN Megan and Abby in the back of the CR-V Adam had driven to Barb's. The two brothers were in front, with Adam at the wheel. Jenny liked looking at him from behind, where she could openly admire his broad shoulders.

Despite a few minor setbacks, the laughter-filled family celebration was right out of her childhood wish book. Jenny felt relaxed and happy, and everyone seemed in good spirits. Even Abby. Ice cream and chocolate sauce had magically erased the discomfort that had abruptly returned when Adam had pressed her to talk.

He'd barely spared Jenny a glance all evening. He hadn't sat beside her or said more than two words to her. She'd missed that, yet she also appreciated his playing smart tonight. None of the Dawsons, and no one at Barb's, could possibly guess that in a little while, Jenny would be in his arms.

They had so much to be thankful for, to celebrate in their own private way. She could hardly wait.

Of course, it all depended on whether Adam could slip away, and Jenny had no problem helping with that. "Feel free to drop your family off before you take me home. That way Abby can get to bed on time," she suggested, figuring Adam would grab at this chance to be alone together.

"Good idea," Megan chimed in. "I'll tuck Abby in for you, Adam. That is, if you don't mind, Abby. I know you like your daddy to do that. But if you let me, I'll read you *two* stories, instead of one."

The little girl nodded.

"Abby says she likes that plan," Megan interpreted.

Drew glanced at his brother, but Adam said nothing. Come to think of it, he'd been especially quiet on the entire drive back.

For the first time, Jenny noted the tension in his shoulders and his stiffly held head. Maybe he was worried about Abby's refusal to attempt speaking in the restaurant. Jenny wasn't at all concerned. No matter how badly the little girl wanted to talk, she wasn't ready. True, she'd uttered two whole words today in front of the handful of students in class, kids who'd shown her nothing but kindness, but she needed time, practice, effort and patience—and lots of it—before she was ready to speak in public.

Jenny wished she'd thought to explain this to Adam this afternoon. She hoped to get the chance when—*if*—they were alone tonight.

The Dawson Ranch sign was a few feet ahead. Adam signaled, then slowed to turn. So they *were* going to have some alone time. Jenny released the breath she'd been holding. Now she could explain about Abby's long road ahead, and suggest that Adam discuss what to expect with Carla Jenson.

Then they'd move on to the more enjoyable business of kissing and caressing. Jenny could hardly wait.

Chapter Thirteen

"Alone at last," Jenny said as the Dawson's back door closed behind Megan, Drew and Abby. Unable to resist touching Adam for one more second, she reached for his hand.

Instead of twining his fingers with hers, he kept a firm two-handed grip on the wheel.

"It's dark, and they're all inside," she said. "I don't think anyone can see us."

"I like to drive with both hands on the wheel."

Did he? Jenny recalled the only other time they'd driven anywhere together, the day he'd helped with the generators. He'd definitely kept both hands on the wheel then—until he parked the truck and kissed her.

In ten minutes, they'd be at her house. She'd just have to hold on a little longer. Adam's attention and affection were certainly well worth the wait. She smiled.

"What're you smiling about?" he asked.

"I was thinking about your hands, and how good you are with them," Jenny teased.

She waited for Adam's responding grin and a suggestive reply. None came. She slanted him a look. "Is everything okay?"

"Why do you ask?"

"Because I know you, Adam. This whole evening, you've hardly said two words to me. At Barb's that made sense, but we're alone now, and you're still barely speaking to me. When you *do* say something, your voice is gruff, and you won't even look at me. I know something is bothering you."

He didn't argue or take his eyes from the road. He definitely was upset.

"This is about Abby at the restaurant, isn't it?" she guessed. "I want you to know that what happened at Barb's tonight—"

"I don't want to discuss that right now—or anything else." Adam flipped on the radio, found a country station and cranked up the volume.

Okay, then. Message received.

Determined not to say another word, at least for the moment, Jenny clamped her lips together.

The CR-V's headlights bounced off the road and splashed the prairie in light, illuminating the dying grass. Beyond that, utter blackness.

While Taylor Swift sang out her heart, Jenny tried to understand the man beside her. The man who last night had been so eager to be with her, so passionate and attentive. This very morning, he'd texted that he was thinking about her and their evening together. This afternoon he'd also seemed fine, pleased for Abby, while his eyes telegraphed his desire for Jenny.

The three of them had been so happy. What had changed in the hours since?

Possible explanations flittered through Jenny's mind. Was Adam upset that she'd spoken up for Abby at the restaurant, that she'd defended his daughter for not attempting to speak?

Or was the cause of his bad mood related to something else entirely? For example, his and Jenny's…Jenny searched for a word to define the discussions and laughter, their secret meetings, the kissing and the give-and-take of pleasure.

Only one word described what they shared. *Relation-*

ship. Not the serious, long-term kind, which neither of them wanted. By tacit agreement, theirs was a here-and-now, no-questions-asked relationship. No, their relationship wasn't the problem.

Then what? Jenny tried to think of other causes for Adam's dark mood, but came up empty.

By the time he pulled to a stop near her front door, she was a bundle of nerves. He kept the engine idling, just as he had that afternoon weeks ago, when they'd made out like high-school kids. Tonight, he seemed in no mood for kissing.

She'd left a lamp on in the living room, and light shone through a gap in the curtains. Not enough light to see Adam clearly, but enough to note the rigid set of his jaw.

On the radio, a twangy male voice lamented his failed love. Jenny wanted to turn the stupid thing off, wanted to demand that Adam talk to her right now, but some sixth sense warned her to be patient and let him take the lead.

With a growing sense of doom, she waited.

When she was about to gnaw off her thumbnail, he finally silenced the radio.

"I don't know how to put this, so I'll just come out and say it straight," he said. "I can't do this anymore."

"Do what?" Jenny asked, but she knew. Adam had lost interest in her, in what they shared. She hugged her purse to her chest.

"After tonight there's bound to be a lot of talk about us," he said. "I don't want one single person to see or hear anything that could fuel that gossip. I don't want my daughter getting the wrong idea and winding up hurt."

"I don't, either, Adam. That's why we never go out together, and why you only come by late at night. Tonight was a special circumstance—a family celebration of Abby's huge milestone. I only came along because she invited me. She wanted me there because I'm her teacher and we've been working so hard together."

He nodded. "And I get that. Neither of us wants to get serious, and we're both okay with that, but I still worry about Abby."

Jenny's first guess had been closer to the mark. This was about Abby, only not in the way she'd thought.

Adam made a good point. For Abby's sake, they probably *should* stop seeing each other. Yet Jenny couldn't imagine that, couldn't imagine life in Saddlers Prairie without Adam to share the highlights of the day with, to hold on to and be held by.

Before she could even think what to say, he dropped his bombshell. "We never should've started up. This…this *thing* between us—it's a big mistake."

JENNY FLINCHED, and Adam knew he'd shocked her with his words, but he'd needed to say them. Not only for his own sake, but for Abby's and Jenny's.

That didn't make them hurt any less. In fact, telling her hurt like hell. But it was better now, before he was totally gone on her, than later.

With her back pressed against the passenger door she faced him, so that her face was in shadow, and she was as far away from him as she could get.

"Since the things we've shared are, in your words, a 'big mistake,' let's just pretend none of it happened," she said tonelessly. "Is that satisfactory?"

She'd reverted to teacher mode, which she did when she wanted to distance herself. Pretending they'd never fooled around wouldn't be easy, but it was better than opening his heart to her.

"Fine. About what happened at Barb's…" Despite her coat and the warm temperature of the CR-V, Jenny chafed her arms. "Don't assume that she'll suddenly become a big talker, because she probably won't. Promise me you'll talk with Carla Jenson right away. She'll explain what Abby, you and the rest of your family need to do from now on and what to expect."

"I was planning to do that in the morning."

"Great. Also, I still expect to see you at our parent-teacher conference next week."

"You sure about that?" Adam wasn't. After tonight, being alone with Jenny was bound to be awkward.

"As Abby's teacher, I want the best for her. We have things to discuss about her progress at school. So, yes, I'm certain."

She really did care about his daughter, and Adam knew that no matter what happened between the two of them, she wouldn't hold any of it against Abby, that she'd put his daughter's well-being first.

For some reason, that hurt even more, like a hard squeeze to the heart. He hid his pain under a terse nod. "I'll be there. Listen, you don't need to drive Abby to Red Deer tomorrow or any other Friday. I totally understand."

"As I've explained before, it's no trouble. Besides, the long drive will give us a chance to practice her speech lessons. There is one thing, though." Jenny nibbled her lip. "If someone could come out to get Abby as soon as I pull up to the house, and if Megan and Mrs. Ames know not to invite me in… I mean, they only did it once, but after tonight, they might again, and… If they know not to, it'll be less uncomfortable for all of us."

Adam couldn't think how to handle that without inviting questions and funny looks, but he'd figure out a way later. "Okay. Anything else?"

"Just…thank you for the ice cream, Adam, and for including me tonight. I had a wonderful—" Jenny's voice broke and she cut herself off. "Good night."

She slipped out of the car, then hurried to the front door.

Feeling like a first-class jerk, Adam rubbed his face with his hands. As soon as she stepped inside, he drove away.

SHORTLY AFTER ADAM STUMBLED into the kitchen early Saturday morning, the rains started. Cold, sleeting sheets of the stuff that could very well turn into snow at any time. The first real sign of the coming winter.

While the coffee brewed, Drew wandered in. Silently they each downed two cups of the high-octane stuff—they'd both worked until late the night before and needed the caffeine jolt—along with several fried-egg sandwiches.

Drew opened the fridge and grabbed the lunches Megan had thoughtfully packed the night before. He tossed one Adam's way. "Let's go."

Relishing the work that was sure to keep his mind off Jenny, Adam headed into the mudroom.

Within moments he and Drew donned waterproof gloves and heavy rain gear. After opting for Stetsons instead of the usual baseball caps, they tromped to Adam's truck. No riding horses today.

Neither spoke as they headed west toward the adjacent fenced holding pastures for a long day of sorting the calves that needed weaning from their mothers. Shortly after they arrived, they were joined by three hands. The rest of the crew were taking care of various other chores.

Neither Adam's heavy-duty rain gear nor his Stetson provided much protection against the nasty weather. Wind propelled icy water down the back of his collar, and before long, he was cold and wet. Which didn't help his lousy mood one bit.

Around noon, the crew broke for lunch, which they took in their vehicles.

Drew and Adam whipped off their gloves and headed for

the truck, Drew blowing on his hands. "Damn, it's cold. I sure wish this sleet would let up for a few hours."

"And I wish every rainbow ended in a pot of gold," Adam grumbled.

"What's that supposed to mean?"

"Wishes are a big load of crap, and complaining only makes life worse."

"Bad moods don't help, either, and yours is a doozy."

Adam kicked a sodden cow patty, sending pieces flying. "What the hell business is that of yours?"

"It's my business when I have to put up with it. You're acting like a real ass, and have been for a few days now. Come to think of it, since the night at Barb's."

His brother's slanted, squinty look galled Adam. He shoved his hands into his jeans pockets and frowned. "You're full of crap."

"I know what I see. What's the deal?" When Adam compressed his lips, Drew snorted. "Not gonna talk, huh? Here's what I think. You tried something when you took Jenny home that night, but she wasn't having any of it. Don't let that stop you, big brother. She wants you."

Just what Adam needed, his brother playing Dr. Phil. He rolled his eyes.

"It's all in the way a woman looks at you," Drew said. "Take Megan. Sometimes her eyes take on a special glow, and her face goes all soft. Then she gets that cute, little smile on her face…" His lips curled into his own smile. "When that happens, I know exactly what she wants, and I make sure she gets it. That's a win-win for both of us."

Jenny might want Adam for fooling around, but nothing more. As they climbed into the truck, he wondered what his brother had seen that made him think Jenny wanted him. He wasn't about to ask. What was the point when he wasn't about to start seeing her again?

"You and Megan think alike and want the same things," he said after he and Drew opened their lunches. "Jenny and I have nothing in common. We don't have any reason to get involved."

"Baloney. You two have plenty in common."

Drew was wrong, and this conversation was over. Adam bit into his sandwich. Yet, after he finished it off and downed the water from his water bottle, he felt the need to hear what Drew had to say. "Exactly what do Jenny and I have in common?"

"For starters, you both care about Abby. And you have chemistry." They opened their doors and headed toward the pasture, the hands following suit. "Any fool with eyes can see that you're hot for each other."

He was right on both counts, but Drew didn't know the dangerous part. That Adam was starting to care, and that neither he nor Jenny wanted Abby to get hurt. Abby was already too close to her and if things didn't work out between him and Jenny... Adam couldn't imagine what that would do to his little girl.

"You should get *your* eyes examined because you need glasses." Adam thwacked his wet gloves hard against his thighs, sending droplets of water flying. "Butt right out of my business."

He stalked away, but Drew caught up to him.

"I'll butt out when you take the stick out of your ass and start acting human again."

Nearby, one of the hands cleared his throat.

Adam skidded to a stop. "I think I'll head back, saddle up and help shuttle some of those calves to the winter pastures. You finish up without me."

"Great idea," Drew said. "Maybe that'll take you mind off your woman troubles. If not, at least you're out of my face."

Adam muttered a few choice words, and then he returned to the truck.

Chapter Fourteen

As much as Jenny enjoyed parent-teacher conferences, when Thursday afternoon rolled around, she was more than ready to finish with the last three meetings. And for a change of weather. For days now, wind and sleet had slashed the windows and roof like angry twins. A fitting tribute for the first anniversary of her father's death this Saturday.

She missed him so much. Especially lately. Sorrow clogged her throat, and tears blurred her eyes. She needed a good cry, but with the first parent due in thirty minutes and lunch still to eat, this was no time to give in to grief. After dabbing her eyes, she adjusted the heat, as the room never seemed quite warm enough. She made a mental note to stop at Spenser's and pick up a few extra space heaters.

Sitting at her desk, she munched her sandwich and thought about the conferences ahead. Unfortunately, the two o'clock was with Adam.

Jenny dreaded facing him, and had the circles under her eyes to prove it. Stress over what to say, and how to act had made for a sleepless night. But she'd been through worse, and survived—coworkers and supposed friends gossiping behind her back, both about her mother and the breakup with Rob. Making her feel like an outcast, instead of a woman who fit in.

The Wylers were tough—that's what Dad always said. During the conference with Adam she intended to prove that.

She'd show him that she was fine, and didn't miss him at all. Which wasn't true, but she'd always been good at pretending that all was right with the world—even when she was a basket case. Adam would never know how badly he'd hurt her the other night.

In a stroke of blind luck, she'd scheduled him between the other two appointments, leaving no time for uncomfortable small talk.

The door opened, and Will and Carol Borden, parents of eighth-grade student Jonas, rushed in, quickly shutting the door behind them.

"It's awful out there," Carol said as she finger-combed her hair. "But that's mid-October—wind, wind and more wind."

"Thank you for coming out in the bad weather." Jenny gestured at the low-lying hooks along the wall. "Please, hang up your coats."

"Have you read this month's book selection, yet?" Carol asked as she and Will sat down.

The next book-club meeting was a week from Saturday. "I'm almost finished with the book," Jenny said. "But we should save our comments about the story and discuss Jonas's progress to date." She slid a copy of the boy's progress report toward Carol and Will.

"This is Jonas's midsemester progress report," she said. "Take a moment to read through it, and then we can discuss any questions you may have."

After both parents raised their gazes from the report, she began. "As you see, Jonas excels in math. He's not as proficient at reading, and to improve his skills, over the rest of the school year I'll be assigning books for him to read, followed by reports about that book. I've made a book list for you."

She handed over the list.

Will Borden, a CPA, looked proud. "I was just like Jonas—not so hot at English and great at math."

Carol glanced fondly at her husband. "That's why you're the best CPA in town."

"The only CPA," he quipped.

"I've told you this before, Carol," Jenny said. "But it bears repeating. Jonas is a real asset to our classroom. He's well-adjusted and helpful with the younger students. I have no doubt he'll do beautifully in high school next year."

"Thanks to you, Jenny," Carol beamed. "He's been telling us about Abby Dawson. What's happening is amazing and so sweet."

Not about to discuss Abby with the couple, even if she did consider Carol a friend, Jenny simply nodded. "The students in my classroom are very supportive of one another. They have been since the first day of school."

As she wrapped up what had been a pleasant forty-five minutes, some sixth sense warned her that Adam was pulling into the parking lot. Stomach churning, she folded her hands on her desk.

She barely had time to gird herself before he strode inside, bringing a gust of icy wind with him, and filling the room with his presence.

Though Jenny's heart tripped, she managed a cool smile.

"Hello, Adam," she said, proud of her polite-but-distant tone. "If you could wait by the door a moment? We're just about finished here. Any last questions, Carol and Will?"

The couple shook their heads, and they all stood.

"Thank you, Jenny," Carol said. "You're doing a great job here. The whole town thinks so. See you a week from Saturday."

"I'll be there, and I appreciate your kind words. Thanks for coming in. If you ever have questions or concerns, don't hesitate to let me know. Drive safely out there."

The Bordens greeted Adam, then shrugged into their coats. By the time the door closed behind them, Adam was seated across the desk, his wool jacket slung over the back of the chair. This was the first time Jenny had seen him with a jacket.

As always, he wore faded jeans, but a flannel shirt replaced the usual T-shirt. The heavy flannel hugged his broad shoulders, and the dark navy color brought out the blue of his eyes.

Water droplets glistened in his hair and on his face. Whereas once Jenny would've reached out and brushed them from his skin, now she clasped her hands tightly on the desk.

Adam couldn't seem to get comfortable. Clearly as ill at ease as Jenny, he shifted around. More than ready to get this over with as quickly as possible, she reached for a pen.

"How are you?" Adam asked.

Under his scrutiny, her calm facade slipped. She was near to crumbling and breaking down. While pretending to search for the manila folder containing Abby's information, Jenny mustered control.

"Saturday is the first anniversary of my father's death," she said. Why had she told him that?

He gave her a sympathetic look. "That's bound to be a rough day. The first anniversary of my father's death, Drew and I brought fresh flowers to his grave. We did the same thing for our Mom. You can't exactly drive over to the Seattle cemetery. What'll you do instead?"

Jenny wasn't sure, but the weekend was bound to be lonely. "I'll probably spend part of the day in quiet reflection, remembering," she said.

"That should work."

For a few moments, only the sleet, wind and the click of the heater filled the silence. If Adam would just quit *scrutinizing* her…

Flustered, she picked up the pen and tapped it on Abby's folder. "I have another conference after yours, so we should probably start. I spoke with Carla on Monday afternoon, and she said that you and she had a nice, long talk."

Adam nodded. "She told me exactly what to do and what to expect from Abby. From now on, we'll be touching base every week. Tuesday she sent home new exercises to practice," he added. "She also decided it was time to drop the Friday lesson. From now on, she'll see Abby only on Tuesdays, so you don't have to drive her to Red Deer anymore."

That meant Jenny now had the entire afternoon off tomorrow, and then the weekend. What should've felt like a glorious minibreak instead loomed like a dark cloud. If only Saddlers Prairie had a movie theater, where she could escape into a comedy or drama Friday night. Any movie would do. She needed something to take her mind off herself. She wished the book club met this Saturday. Maybe if the weather improved by Sunday, she'd drive around and explore more of the area beyond Saddlers Prairie.

She managed a smile. "I'll miss the extra time with Abby, but that's good news."

She opened Abby's folder, slid the report across the desk, and gave Adam the same spiel as she had the Bordens.

The difference with this appointment, though, was that Jenny couldn't observe Adam without pain. She wasn't about to wonder why a man she didn't love could hurt her so badly. While he looked over the report, she glanced at the notes she'd scribbled. She didn't need them, but studying them was better than sitting here, looking everywhere but at him.

"She's doing okay, then," Adam said after scanning the report.

"Abby's been working hard in class," she said, keeping her gaze on her notes. "She knows all her letters—at least, I think she does. When I ask, she always points out the right one, and sometimes tells me the name of the letter. We're working on pronunciation. Some letters are more challenging than others, but I have no doubt that by the end of the semester, she'll be able to say them all."

Adam nodded. "What about the minus sign under social skills?"

"As you know, she doesn't socialize with other children. We're working on that, too, though. I encourage everyone to treat her like a normal little girl. Halloween is a week from Monday, and the Spensers mentioned throwing a party for all the students. Any day now, Abby should get her invitation in the mail. I hope she'll decide to go."

"I'll work on convincing her." Adam cleared his throat. "I appreciate all that you're doing. And that you aren't holding what happened between us against my daughter."

"I'd never do that!" Realizing that her temper and her voice had risen, Jenny sucked in a calming breath. "No need to thank me, Adam," she said, in an easier tone. "It's my job."

"What Will and Carol said about you—it's true. You're a good teacher."

"But not good enough for you," Jenny replied, forgetting she wanted to keep her cool. "You think being with me was a big mistake."

Adam swore. "I didn't say that, Jenny. I said that what we were *doing* was a big mistake."

"Tomato, tomah-to."

Adam swore. "Why can't—"

The door blew open, and Anita Eden dashed inside. Her gaze darted from Adam to Jenny, her eyes widening a fraction. "Why can't Jenny what?" Anita asked with a sly smile.

"You eavesdropped," Adam said, not looking pleased.

Under his glare, the woman's sly look vanished. But not her pluck. "Hey, I can't help it if your voices are louder than the wind," she retorted. "Just look at you two. So much animosity. I could cut the tension with a pair of shears."

"Why don't you stick your shears where the sun don't shine instead," he muttered.

"Hush, Adam!" Jenny warned in a low voice.

"Anita, if you could please wait by the door until Adam and I finish that would be great," Jenny told the nosy woman.

"Fine, but I could've sworn you two had something going. That night at Barb's, the way you looked at each other..."

"We never looked at each other, not once," Adam said.

Anita shrugged. "Not at the same time."

"Perhaps you should take up fiction writing," Jenny replied, none too kindly. "There's nothing between Adam and me. Nothing at all." She returned to Adam. "Any other questions before you leave?"

"Nope."

"Thank you for coming this afternoon." With another fake smile, Jenny dismissed him. As the door closed behind him, she let out a relieved breath.

"Who shall we discuss first, Julie or Edgar?" she asked when Anita sat down.

Once she started a serious discussion of the hairdresser's son and daughter, Anita dropped her busybody act.

When Jenny finished pointing out the strengths and weaknesses of both children, Anita's own troubles poured out. Divorced, she struggled to make ends meet at her beauty salon. Donna helped when possible, but she wasn't exactly rolling in cash, either. Anita was lonely, too, and in search of a good man.

Jenny didn't mind hearing the story. She understood the woman better now, and actually liked her.

After ninety minutes, Jenny had heard enough and was ready to wrap up. "Thank you for coming, Anita," she said, signaling the end of the conference.

"Before I go, there is one more thing I need to say." Anita leaned forward. "Adam Dawson is well-off and handsome. If you're not interested, I'll take him."

Adam with Anita...Jenny didn't like the idea. But he didn't want Jenny, and since she didn't want anything serious with him.... She had no right to be upset or possessive.

"He's not mine to give," she said.

"Ah, well, he's not interested in me anyway. Never has been, and believe me, I've tried to catch his eye since fourth grade." Anita shrugged. "Later I got married and he went off to college and did the same thing. Then Simone died, and I got divorced. I waited for a few years before I tried again. After all, a man deserves to mourn in peace. By then, Adam had his hands full with Abby and the ranch. But the truth is, since Simone died, he hasn't even looked at a woman, let alone dated. Until you came to town."

Any interest he had in Jenny had died a quick death. But she wasn't about to share with Anita, who was after all, a gossip.

"We should wrap up now." Jenny stood, giving Anita a smile to cover her desire to get the woman to leave.

Anita also rose. "I've been around the block a few times, and I know men," she said as she slipped into her coat. "Trust me, you're the one Adam wants."

AFTER ANITA LEFT, JENNY turned off the heat and straightened the room, all the while puzzling over the hairdresser's words. How could she possibly think Adam wanted Jenny when he so obviously didn't? He could barely even look at her.

She thought about the weekend that loomed ahead. Spending the day alone on the anniversary of her father's death was bad enough, but Friday afternoon and Sunday, too?

Never mind, she'd keep busy. Grocery shopping, then lunch at Barb's. She sighed. That would eat up all of an hour and a half. Maybe she'd invite Megan and some of her other new friends over for coffee Saturday afternoon.

Adam would probably have a fit over that. Regardless of *his* negative feelings for Jenny, Megan liked her. They were becoming good friends—even if Jenny couldn't share what had happened between her and Adam.

She was about to shrug into her coat and flip out the lights, when her cell chirped. She didn't recognize the name on the screen, but decided to pick up anyway.

"This is Rodney Biss from *Billings Daily News*," said a man with a deep voice. "I'm looking for Jenny Wyler."

After the story that had run in the Seattle paper, Jenny didn't trust reporters. Wary, she frowned. "What do you want?"

If her rudeness bothered the man, he didn't show it. "I'm doing a series on one-room schools in America, and your name came up. I'd like to interview you."

"Oh, really?" Jenny sank onto the corner of her desk. "And just how did you hear about me?"

"From an old acquaintance, a woman named Phylinda Graham."

At the mention of Miss Graham, Jenny relaxed. "I'm flattered, but did she mention that I've only been teaching here since September?"

"She did. The series profiles several one-room schools across the country, and the teachers who staff them. Most have been at the job for years. With your background, coming from a large school district into a one-room school, you'll bring an interesting perspective, one I believe my readers will enjoy. I'm happy to send you links to the articles that have run so far."

That sounded all right. "Please do," Jenny said. "Why don't you call me back next week, and we'll do the interview then."

"I'd like to drive over for a face-to-face meeting instead, if that works for you. That way, I can take a few photos of the school and of you with your kids."

Her students would have the chance to meet a newspaper reporter. Jenny's mind spun with ideas for a lesson plan on print journalism. "Do you think you could stay and answer some questions from the students?"

"For a little while, sure."

"I'll have to okay any pictures with the parents, but that sounds great."

They set a day and time, then hung up.

Jenny was scribbling the information on her calendar when her cell rang again.

This time the caller was Phylinda Graham.

Smiling, she answered. "Hello, Miss Graham."

"Hello, dear," said the cultured voice. "I wanted to alert you that I gave your name to a *Billings Daily News* reporter named Rodney Biss. I met him years ago when he covered a teachers convention in Billings, and we've kept in touch."

"As a matter of fact, we just spoke."

"Did you schedule the interview?"

"Yes, for next Wednesday. I'm curious—why did you give him my name?"

"Because you impressed me, dear. How's the teaching coming along?"

"I just finished my midsemester parent-teacher conferences this afternoon," Jenny said. "I happen to have tomorrow afternoon free. If you're in the mood for company, I'd love to come visit and catch you up."

"That would be lovely. Why don't you come for dinner?"

They chatted a few more minutes. When they hung up, Jenny was smiling.

Already the weekend was looking up.

Chapter Fifteen

Bowing her head against the harsh wind, Jenny hurried into the lobby of Sunset Manor. As before, Phylinda Graham was waiting for her.

"Goodness, what a blustery evening," she said. "I'm glad you made it safely."

As Jenny smoothed her hair and shrugged out of her coat, rain began to patter the windows. "Apparently just in time."

"According to the news, we're in for a bit of nasty weather. Our first snow could come anytime now."

"That'd be better than this freezing rain and nonstop wind."

"Once you experience that first blizzard, you may change your mind. But enough about the weather." Miss Graham hooked her arm through Jenny's. "Our dinner reservation is for six, and it's just that now. Shall we head into the dining room?"

As before, the room was packed. This time, Miss Graham introduced Jenny to several of the diners.

"Your friends seem nice," Jenny said as they sat down at their table.

The older woman smiled. "They're all interesting people. I thought about inviting them to join us this evening, but I want you to myself. I want to hear all about you and school. Oh, look, here's our waitress."

"I had a lovely chat with Carla Jenson's mother the other day," Miss Graham said after they ordered their meals. "She shared the most wonderful news—that Abby Dawson has started talking."

"Yes, and isn't that amazing?" Jenny grinned. "I'm sorry I didn't call and let you know. I've been…" She paused. How could she sum up all that had happened without going into the embarrassing details? "Distracted," she said. "Thank you so much for referring the Dawsons to Carla. Without her help, Abby might never have spoken."

"Don't discount your own influence, dear. Under your nurturing hand, that little girl could very well have spoken on her own."

Warm words, indeed. "We'll never know," Jenny said. "What matters is that she's making slow-but-steady progress."

The salads arrived. After sampling the greens, Jenny's dinner companion set down her fork. "What did you mean, 'distracted'?"

Silently chastising herself for her word choice, Jenny gave a vague wave. "Personal things."

Miss Graham regarded her with a shrewd look. "I sense a melancholy about you that seems new."

"You're right," Jenny said. "Tomorrow is the first anniversary of my father's death."

"I'm sorry, dear." Miss Graham patted Jenny's hand.

"Thanks. I miss him a lot."

"I'm sure you do, and I know he'd be proud of what you're doing here." After a moment, the older woman glanced at Jenny, a glint in her eye. "Are there other distractions? Man troubles?"

Jenny's jaw dropped. "How did you know that?"

"I'm good at reading people, and you're an open book."

Jenny filled her mouth with salad so that she couldn't reply. Long ago, she'd learned to never project her true feelings, and had always prided herself on being hard to read. How and when had that changed?

"Don't be alarmed, dear. I speak as a friend who only wants to help." Miss Graham's wise, brown eyes were warm with concern.

From out of nowhere, the need to talk about Adam and what had happened reared up, the words crowding Jenny's throat so that she could barely swallow her food.

She *needed* a friendly ear, someone she could trust. She couldn't very well confide in Megan or any of her new friends in town, not about this.

The waitress delivered the meal. As soon as she left, Jenny leaned closer to Miss Graham and lowered her voice. "Promise you'll keep what I say to yourself."

"This goes no further than the two of us. You have my word."

Satisfied, Jenny began, "It's Adam Dawson." While they ate, she filled Miss Graham in, omitting only the physical intimacies she and Adam had shared.

"We never made any promises to each other, and had only been seeing each other a few weeks," she finished. "I thought we were getting along really well. Then suddenly Adam changed his mind. It was all so abrupt."

"That must have hurt."

Emotions Jenny had no desire to share threatened to bubble up. Struggling for control, she rearranged her napkin across her lap.

"You do understand that Adam was devastated when Simone died," Miss Graham said.

Jenny nodded. "I've been hurt, too. Nothing like Adam, of course. The truth is, I can't afford to get involved. I'm only here until the end of the school year. Adam doesn't know that, and neither does anyone else but you. There are also other reasons for not getting involved, most especially Abby. Neither of us wants her to get hurt. I won't go into the rest. What I'm trying to say is that I know Adam's change of heart is for the best." She should count her blessings he'd pulled away, saving them both from pain and heartache. Yet, despite all common sense, a part of her wanted to be with him. "So why does it hurt?"

"Because you have feelings for him."

Jenny started to shake her head, then sighed and admitted what she'd kept even from herself. "I suppose I do. But I don't want to."

"Your heart doesn't care a whit about that."

They returned to their meal, though Jenny barely tasted anything. She was too scared. She'd never meant to care about Adam or anyone in Saddlers Prairie.

"Setting matters of the heart aside for the moment, are you sure you want to leave Saddlers Prairie at the end of the school year?" Miss Graham asked.

Now more than ever. "That's always been my plan," Jenny said.

"Plans definitely have their place in our lives." Miss Graham's eyebrows lifted delicately. "But what do you *want?*"

While the waitress cleared their plates and served dessert, Jenny mulled over the question. She genuinely liked her students and her job. Most everyone she'd met in Saddlers Prairie was warm and friendly, and the wide-open spaces appealed to her. Best of all, no one knew a thing about her mother.

Miss Graham was nibbling a butter cookie, and clearly awaiting Jenny's reply.

"The truth is, I don't know what I want," she conceded. "It's only the third week of October. I don't have to make up my mind for a while."

"In fairness to the school, you ought to let them know by

the end of first semester. Last year's teacher left them hanging until it was almost too late to find you."

Miss Graham was right.

"Abby and the other children would benefit greatly if you stayed," she continued. "Perhaps you should think about that."

"I will," Jenny vowed. So much to think about.

They finished their cookies in silence. A particularly loud gust of wind rattled the windows.

Miss Graham looked worried. "The wind just keeps getting worse. If I know Montana, the temperature is dropping, too. The roads are probably icing up. You should get home, while you still can."

After promising to call her friend again soon, Jenny was ready to drive home, relax and forget about everything for the weekend. She would not think about Adam Dawson or whether to stay in Saddlers Prairie. Or anything of any consequence, until tomorrow when she would remember her father. Tonight, climbing into bed and curling up with a mystery novel while the storm ran its course sounded good.

She turned onto the highway. The rain had stopped, but the wind had intensified to the point that holding the car steady was a real challenge. Mindful of Miss Graham's warning about ice on the road, Jenny gripped the wheel and moved at a snail's pace. She didn't even switch on the radio. Her entire focus was on arriving home in one piece.

She didn't draw in a deep breath or release her death grip on the wheel until she turned onto Pinto Road. Her hands ached from squeezing the wheel so hard.

Snow began to swirl through the air, wind-whipped and wild in the headlights. Home in the nick of time, she thought.

The house was dark when she drove up. Odd. She'd left the living room and porch lights on. The power must be out. Thank goodness for the generator out back, and for Adam's help. All she needed was a flashlight so that she could see to start it.

The wind was so strong, she struggled to open the car door. Bowing her head against the gusts, she made her way forward. Before reaching the front stoop, Jenny fished the house key from her purse.

Something made her glance upward. What she saw stole her breath. The tree out back had crashed into the roof.

BACK FROM DOING A QUICK check on things, Adam trudged into the mudroom Friday night. He hung up his coat, whacked the snow from his gloves and yanked off his boots. The horses were settled and warm in the barn, and the cattle were holding their own against the snow and raging wind. Barring an emergency, he could relax until morning.

Bone weary, he was relieved to be through for the night. With Drew and Megan upstairs, and Abby snug in bed, he had the family room to himself.

He was munching one of Mrs. Ames's chewy, chocolate brownies and channel-surfing when the landline in the kitchen rang. Colin, any of the ranchers, and just about everyone knew to call the cell if something was wrong, but just in case...

Muttering, Adam pushed to his feet. He wasn't halfway to the kitchen before the ringing stopped. If it was important, they'd call back.

He took the phone with him to the family room in time to catch Drew and Megan hurrying down the stairs.

"I thought you two were in bed," Adam quipped.

"We were getting there." Drew buttoned his shirt and tucked it in. "Then the phone rang."

"I tried to answer, but you must've beat me to it," Adam said. "I'm surprised you lovebirds even heard the thing."

Neither Megan nor Drew smiled.

Warning bells sounded in Adam's head. "What's happened? Who called?"

"Silas Mason, with bad news. Apparently the wind ripped up the cottonwood in Jenny's backyard. Her roof is in bad shape."

Dear God. Adam stood. "She okay?"

"Luckily she wasn't inside when it happened. I'm heading over there now to help Silas and some other men lay down a tarp and try to keep the snow out of the house and the damage down."

Adam was already on his way to the mudroom. "Keep an eye on Abby for me, Megan. You know how soundly she sleeps, so that shouldn't be a problem."

His sister-in-law shook her head. "I'm coming with you. Just give me a minute to let Mrs. Ames know."

By the time Adam and Drew loaded the truck with equipment they might need, the housekeeper was in the kitchen filling a thermos with hot cocoa.

Moments later, Drew and Megan squeezed into the passenger side of the truck and Adam roared off.

THE WIPERS WAGED A HARD BATTLE against the wind and snow. Heart in his throat, Adam turned into Jenny's place. Half a dozen vehicles littered the drive and lawn. Someone had started the generator and set up floodlights, bathing the cottage in brilliant, stark light and eerie shadows.

One glimpse of the huge tree and gaping hole where the roof had been, and Adam's breath caught in his chest. If Jenny'd been in there...

A chill that had nothing to do with the freezing temperatures shivered up his back. He silently offered a prayer of thanks.

A power saw buzzed to life as several men worked to clear

away the huge tree. Silas was standing with John Nestor, the insurance agent, who no doubt was assessing the damages.

Adam didn't see Jenny anywhere. Anxious to reach her, he slid from the truck.

"Where are you going?" Drew asked.

"To find Jenny."

Off to the side, he spotted her car. No lights were on, but the engine was running. He strode toward it.

She was sitting inside, hugging herself, her attention riveted to the house.

Feelings Adam didn't want, had tried hard to stamp out, flooded him. He tapped on the window and waited for her to lower it.

"You okay?" he asked, leaning down to shield her from the wind and snow.

Eyes big as quarters, she nodded. "They say the kitchen and bathroom are the only parts of the cottage that aren't damaged. I peeked through the front door." She swallowed hard. "It looks like a war zone in there. Oh, Adam, my house."

The fierce need to comfort and protect her overpowered him. To hell with safeguarding his own feelings or what other people thought. Adam opened the car door, pulled Jenny out and held her.

His jacket was unzipped, and she burrowed close. Through the padding of her thick coat, he felt her shaking.

"You cold?" he said, cupping her head against his chest.

"No. Yes. I don't know."

She must be in shock. Adam tugged the hood of her coat over her head. He rubbed her back. "The main thing is, you're safe."

She sighed. "Now I am."

His chest expanded in relief, spreading warmth through

his body. He rested his chin on her head and closed his eyes, and for one long moment pretended that she was his.

Seconds later, he spotted Megan, standing out of the way, giving him and Jenny privacy. No telling what she must be thinking.

Crazy damned fool. He let go of her, stepped back and nodded for his sister-in-law to come over.

"I'm going to help Silas and the others now," he told Jenny. "But Megan's here." He opened the car door. "Get back in there, where it's warm. She'll sit with you."

Megan had wisely grabbed a thermos with hot cocoa. When Adam joined the other men, she was pouring a cup for Jenny.

Hours and a good three inches of snow accumulation later, the tree was gone, a protective tarp in the hole it had left in Jenny's roof. John Nestor had snapped all the photos he needed and assessed the damage inside and out.

Adam dusted the snow from his shoulders and sleeves. He hung around long enough to suggest that the team he and Drew had used to rebuild the barn on the annexed property fix the damage to Jenny's place.

Then he tromped through the snow and grabbed a flashlight from the truck. "I'm going inside to check the damage," he said.

"Careful in there," Silas warned.

John seconded that, but no one tried to stop Adam. Mindful of where he stepped, he wiped his feet on the mat—funny given the situation—and entered the house.

Roofing debris and small tree branches littered the living room and bedroom, and with every footstep, the carpet bled water. The sofa and chair were just as wet. Jenny's ceramic collection was damp but intact. The damage stopped mere inches from the dining table outside the kitchen. The table, the laptop sitting on it and the kitchen itself were dry and clean.

In the tiny pantry, Adam found a plastic crate and some towels. With fingers numbed by the cold, he dried, wrapped and carefully packed each ceramic object into the crate. He added the laptop and set everything by the front door.

When he glanced out, every man but Drew and him had left.

"What are you doing in there?" Drew asked.

"Jenny will need some things and a change of clothes since she can't stay here."

Drew followed him inside, swearing as he glanced around. They headed for the bedroom.

"I'll do the dresser, you take the closet," Adam said.

A scant moment later, Drew poked his head out of the closet. "Everything in here is a sodden mess, but nothing a good washing and drying won't fix. I'll take the clothes to the truck."

While Drew made several trips, Adam opened the lower dresser drawers and pulled out sweaters, jeans and socks. The top drawer was filled with panties and bras, some of them plain cotton, others lacy and silky soft in his hands.

He recognized one of the bras, a little wisp of satin and lace. He'd seen Jenny in it, her breasts proud and peaked from his attention. Swallowing, he stuffed the sexiest delicates into his back pockets. The rest he slipped between the sweaters.

Drew returned. "All the clothes from the closet are now in the truck. How're you doing?"

"I finished the dresser, but I haven't checked the bathroom yet."

"You do that while I take what you have out," Drew said. "Thanks."

Like the kitchen, the bathroom was untouched. Adam

pulled a neatly folded pillowcase from the linen closet and deposited Jenny's toothpaste, deodorant and cosmetics into it.

He pulled a robe and flannel nightgown from the hook on the back of the bathroom door. Armed with the bulky pillowcase and the crate of ceramics, he exited the cottage. The snow and wind had all but stopped, and the sky was now studded with stars.

Megan and Drew were piling the clothing from the dresser into the trunk of Jenny's car, but Jenny was headed toward the house.

"Whoa, there," Adam said. "Where are you going?"

"I want to go inside." She raised her chin, looking determined and brave. And utterly vulnerable.

She was in no shape to see the extent of the damage. Adam stepped in front of her, blocking her way. "No, Jenny. Not tonight."

"You and Drew did."

"To get some of your things. Wait until daylight. You can go in then."

"All right." She sighed wearily. "What's in the crate?"

"Your laptop and the ceramics from the curio."

"Don't tell me—everything's ruined."

Adam shook his head. "You got lucky. The ceramics were wet, but without so much as a scratch on any of them. Your computer was on the dining table, and it's okay, too."

"Really? I was sure… That's amazing." Her eyes filled. "Thank you, Adam."

The last thing he needed right now was a blubbering woman. "Open the door to the backseat of your car, will you?" he growled, his voice thick with emotion.

She returned to the car and pulled the door open with hands that still shook.

Adam set the box on the seat, and tossed the robe and nightgown beside it. He thought about adding the bras and panties from his pockets, but wasn't about to do that. Not in front of prying eyes.

The trunk slammed shut, and Drew and Megan joined him and Jenny.

"I spoke with John Nestor and know that he assessed the damage, but what happens now?" she asked.

"If you talked to John, you know he okayed the repairs. I recommended the men who rebuilt our barn for the job. They're good people and need work. Silas will call them in the morning, and I expect they'll start first thing Monday."

Jenny gnawed her thumbnail. "How long do you think it'll take to fix everything?"

"With the weather we're having? A good week, maybe longer."

Groaning, she buried her face in her hands. "Where am I supposed to live until then? Is there a motel in town?"

"Forget that," Megan said. "We have room at the ranch. You'll stay with us."

Jenny caught her lip between her teeth. "Are you sure you want me there?" she asked, her gaze on Adam.

Tonight something inside him had shifted. Jenny's well-being was more important than his own need to keep his distance. She felt safe with him, a responsibility he took seriously.

She would feel just as safe in his home. Adam intended to make sure of that. For his sake and his daughter's, he wouldn't touch Jenny, wouldn't even think about wanting her.

He nodded. "I'll call Mrs. Ames and ask her to make up the guest bed."

Chapter Sixteen

Warm from a long soak in a gorgeous claw-foot tub, Jenny settled into an armchair in her temporary bedroom wearing her own nightgown and robe, a steaming mug of tea in her hands.

Megan, who was seated in a matching chair with her own mug, offered a friendly smile. "I hope you'll be comfortable here."

In the soft light of the bedside table lamp, Jenny glanced at the four-poster bed with its white, down comforter. She dug her toes into the thick oval rug that softened the polished oak floor.

"I'm sure I will be. Thank you for inviting me into your home."

"We're happy to have you."

Was Adam? Jenny had no idea. Since arriving at the house, he'd stuck around long enough to show her to her room and deposit her things on the dresser. He'd also pointed out the bathroom she would share with him and Abby, which was sure to be an inconvenience for them. Then he'd turned in. So had Drew. Now, at close to midnight, Jenny and Megan were the only ones awake.

Megan yawned. No doubt, she was exhausted. Jenny was tired, as well, but still too shaken to sleep.

"Don't feel like you have to sit up with me," she said.

"I want to. This is fun, like a sleepover." Megan sipped her tea. "Besides, Drew and I always sleep in on weekends."

"What about Adam? When does he get to sleep in?" Jenny wondered.

"He's welcome to do that Sunday morning—Drew and I have offered enough, but since we got married and I moved in, he never has."

Jenny mulled over that interesting tidbit.

"I'm glad you're here," Megan went on, "and that we're friends."

"Me, too," Jenny said. "Funny, I was thinking of inviting you over to my place for coffee tomorrow. Instead, I'm *here*, in this big, beautiful bedroom."

Jenny gestured at the off-white walls, where oil paintings of the prairie in each of the four seasons hung. "Those are wonderful."

"Aren't they? They were painted right here on the ranch by Drew and Adam's mom. Apparently she was quite the artist."

"I'll say. Did you know her?"

Megan shook her head. "By the time I met Drew, both his parents were gone. I think they must've been fine people. They sure raised great sons."

Jenny glanced at the crate that held her ceramics. That Adam had taken the time and thought to collect and carefully wrap her most treasured possessions… She was still amazed by his thoughtfulness.

Megan followed her gaze. "My brother-in-law tends to be gruff and sometimes short," she said, "but inside, he's a good man."

With a heart of gold.

At dinner tonight, Miss Graham had been so right—Jenny definitely had feelings for Adam Dawson. Strong feelings she'd never expected to experience again, and didn't dare express. Not to Adam or Megan.

Jenny took a long pull of her tea.

Tonight she'd also realized that Adam had feelings for her. By the way he held her and the tender look in his eyes that was obvious.

Under normal circumstances, this would've been dizzying news, enough to make her giddy with joy. Unfortunately, there was nothing normal about Jenny's situation. She couldn't have a serious relationship without explaining about her mother's illness, but even the thought of doing so made her cringe.

Adam was sure to run in the opposite direction, just as Rob had. He'd never look at her in the same warm and tender way again, would regard her with coolness or, worse, contempt. Jenny shivered. She couldn't bear that.

More important, she didn't want to hurt Adam or Abby, which was bound to happen if they got seriously involved.

And that was why he could never know how deeply she cared for him.

"The talk about Mr. and Mrs. Dawson Senior has you thinking about your own father, doesn't it?" Megan said, misinterpreting Jenny's brooding silence. "Adam mentioned that tomorrow is the anniversary of his death." She reached out and touched Jenny's arm. "I'm so sorry."

"Thanks. I'm okay, though. Really."

"Adam said that tomorrow you planned to take time to remember your father. Tell us when, and we'll leave you alone. Or if you'd rather share stories or memories, we'll support you. We're here for you, so let us know what you want."

"That's very kind," Jenny said, knowing she wouldn't share anything. Tired at last, she yawned.

Megan did the same. "If that isn't a signal for turning in." She stood. "If you need anything, Adam is right down the hall, and Drew and I are at the far end. Sleep well, Jenny. And sleep late."

As soon as Megan shut the bedroom behind her, Jenny shed her robe and crawled into bed. She flipped off the bed-side table lamp.

The soft sheets felt luxurious, and the mattress was firm and comfortable. Quiet shrouded the room, as peaceful as the thick comforter on the bed. Perfect for sleep.

Only her mind rebelled. Thoughts spun every which way, ruining any chance of settling down. With a weary sigh, she rose again. Feeling her way around, she padded to the window, opened the drapes and stared out.

In the scant moonlight, the snow near the house was easy to make out. Beyond that, only blackness, which was nothing different from the few other times she'd come here.

The sky was a different matter. After days of wind, rain and tonight's brief snowstorm, the clouds had disappeared. The sliver of moon and scattered stars spilled across the velvety night.

It was a beautiful sight, and somehow soothing. "If you're out there, Dad, know that I'm doing okay," Jenny murmured, feeling a bit silly talking to him. "And that I miss you terribly. I'm going back to the cottage tomorrow, and I hope to find the picture of you, Becca and me that was on my bed-side table. You know the one. Wish me luck. Good night."

Feeling oddly better now and ready to sleep, Jenny left the drapes open, climbed back into bed and snuggled under the covers.

Unfortunately, the instant she closed her eyes, images filled her mind. Of the huge tree, crashed into what had been her roof, and the destruction she'd glimpsed through the front door. Her eyes popped open. "Think happy thoughts," she whispered in desperation.

She turned her mind to her students, Miss Graham, the budding friendship with Megan and the other women in her book club, but nothing soothed her ragged nerves. If only

Adam would hold her like he had outside the cottage. In the warmth and safety of his arms, her worries had faded for a little while.

Jenny half hoped he'd sneak into her room tonight, but she knew he wouldn't.

She fell asleep clutching the spare pillow and longing for him.

ADAM WOKE UP A GOOD HOUR before the alarm was due to go off. Hoping to fall back to sleep, he closed his eyes. Then he remembered—Jenny was in the guest bedroom down the hall. He pictured her lying in that big bed, her light brown hair spread across the snow-white pillow, her lips parted slightly in sleep.

Just like that, his body hardened and ached, urging him to slip into her room and join her. He'd wake her up with a long, deep kiss, watch her lashes flutter open, her sleepy eyes lit with need. Smiling a slow, seductive smile, she'd pull him down for more, her body soft and yielding under him...

About to lose control all by his lonesome, Adam groaned and shut out the thoughts. *Not gonna happen, buddy. No how, no way.*

Muttering a few choice words, he tossed the covers aside and swung his legs over the bed. After a cold shower that gave him gooseflesh but did nothing to cool down his body, he dressed.

When he stepped into his jeans, he realized that Jenny's lingerie was still jammed into the rear pockets. He pulled out the skimpy bras and panties and got hard all over again as though he was some idiot kid instead of a man who knew better.

Dammit. He'd best get rid of them. Now. With no one awake but him, this was the perfect time.

Adam tiptoed barefoot down the hall. He couldn't just

leave the stuff in plain sight, where Abby or Drew or Megan would see them. He needed a paper sack or something to hide them in. He was thinking about where to find a small bag when Jenny's door opened.

Looking sleepy, her hair tangled and in her eyes, she gaped at him. "What are you—"

Adam covered her mouth with his hand. "Shh. Everyone's asleep."

Her lips burned his palm, and for the hundredth time, his body stirred. The instant Jenny nodded, he dropped his hand and stepped back.

She was wearing the flannel nightgown he'd taken from her bathroom. A thick, baggy affair that hid everything except the upper curve of her breasts. For some unfathomable reason that was sexier than any slinky teddy.

Swallowing and willing his hardening body to behave— as if *that* worked—Adam held the lingerie at arm's length. "These are yours," he gruffed in a low voice.

He dropped the items into her hand, turned on his heel and hightailed his way down the stairs.

BARELY AWAKE AND NOT QUITE sure what had just happened, Jenny deposited the lingerie on the bed. Her thoughts on her beloved father, gone exactly one year now, she slipped into her robe, then headed for the bathroom, which she'd been about to visit when she'd caught Adam outside her door.

Clutching her sexiest bras and panties in his big hand. If that wasn't strange…

After using the facilities and making herself presentable— her hair had been a disaster, and her breath not much better— she set her grief aside and moved quietly down the stairs to find out what he'd been up to.

Following the smell of freshly brewed coffee, she entered

the kitchen. Adam was standing near the coffeemaker, clearly waiting for his caffeine.

"Coffee's almost ready."

By his frown, he was less than thrilled by her company. Or maybe he was embarrassed about the lingerie.

Jenny crossed her arms. "What were you doing outside my room with my underwear?"

Adam glanced at his feet. "It's not what you might think. I put those bras and panties in my pockets last night, and forgot to give them to you."

"You've had them since last night," she repeated. "In your pockets."

"They're pretty skimpy, and I didn't want Drew looking at them, so I stashed them where he wouldn't look." His ears reddened.

Jenny was charmed by that, and she stifled a smile. "So you were just going to leave them at my door?"

"Something like that. I didn't mean to wake you." Adam opened a cabinet and pulled out two mugs.

"I wasn't asleep."

"It's early for you to be up. Bad night?"

She nodded. "Every time I closed my eyes, I saw the tree and the hole in the roof. I kept thinking about that mess, and what I'd lost." Though Jenny's robe and the kitchen were toasty warm, she shivered. She wanted to move into Adam's arms for a comforting hug, but he didn't offer. He wouldn't even meet her eyes. Maybe he was embarrassed about the underwear.

"The whole thing sucks, that's for sure," he said.

The coffeemaker gurgled to a stop. He filled the mugs, then set her coffee on the built-in cutting board as if wanting to avoid even the touch of her hand.

"Milk's in the fridge," he said. "Sugar's on the table."

"Thanks." After adding milk to her drink, Jenny sat down.

She expected Adam to join her, but he remained standing, his hips canted against the counter. He was dressed in jeans and a long-sleeve wool shirt, but his feet were bare. What was it about the sight of his bare feet that endeared her so?

Uncomfortable silence hung between them.

Jenny added sugar and searched her mind for something to say. "I guess I'll go to the cottage later this morning, and see what I can salvage," she said.

"You should take someone with you."

"Why?"

"It's pretty bad in there. You might want company."

"I'm a big girl, Adam. I can handle this alone." Jenny changed the subject. "Megan said she and Drew get to sleep in this morning. What exactly do you do around the ranch at this hour?"

"Feed the horses. Drive around the ranch, checking on cattle, the river and any downed fence." Adam shrugged. "Stuff like that."

"I thought you had a foreman and crew to do those things."

"Now and then, they deserve to sleep in, too."

"And you don't?"

"I get what I need." He downed his coffee in one gulp.

He seemed so hostile that Jenny wondered if she'd imagined his caring and concern last night. But no, the warmth in his eyes, the tender way he'd held her had been real.

Facing him now, she saw the truth. Adam *didn't* care about her the way she thought—he'd have reacted with the same solicitous warmth to anyone in her position. That must be the reason for his distance now. He didn't want her thinking he was interested.

Jenny raised her chin. "Adam, I want you to know that I understand about last night. I was upset, and I'm grateful to you for being there for me. But that's all it was, comfort. I know you don't want to be more than friends, and I... I'm just fine with that."

She expected to see relief on his face, but his expression was blank, and she had no idea what he was thinking.

"I figured as much." Adam drained his mug and set it in the sink. "I'd best see to those chores. Abby usually sleeps until seven-thirty, but if she comes down early, could you turn on the cartoon channel in the family room? Tell her that when I get back, I'll make pancakes."

Before Jenny so much as nodded, he was gone.

Chapter Seventeen

By the time Adam steered the truck toward the house, the sun was up and most of last night's snow had melted. Checking on the ranch had kept him busy, and for a while he'd managed to forget about Jenny.

Now thoughts of her flooded his mind. Their conversation this morning in the kitchen, telling him she couldn't sleep for her worries. She'd looked as vulnerable as she had last night, and he'd wanted to pull her close and comfort her as he had then. But that was a bad idea, and he'd managed to keep his hands off her. Barely.

The last thing she needed was for some lust-crazed man who'd promised to keep her safe to lose control. Especially when, as she'd so aptly reminded him, the physical part of their relationship was over.

Yeah, he'd been the one to end it, but now he wanted to ignore all common sense and start it up again.

Hoping like hell that she was upstairs and out of sight, Adam stopped in the mudroom and hung up his jacket. As he settled onto the bench to pull off his boots, the soft sounds of feminine laughter—Abby's and Jenny's—rippled toward him.

He wanted in on the fun, wanted to laugh right along with them. If he meant to keep his distance, though, that wasn't smart, and he considered shoving his feet back into the boots and heading out again.

Suddenly he remembered. Today was the first anniversary of the death of Jenny's father.

And he hadn't said a single word this morning.

Nice going, Dawson.

He padded into the kitchen. Jenny was dressed in jeans and a pullover, sitting at the table with Abby. His daughter wore a sweater and jeans, too. Someone, probably Jenny, had fixed her hair. They were reading the Saturday comics in the *Billings Daily News,* which most people in town subscribed to, and drinking orange juice.

"Morning, ladybug." He pulled one of Abby's pigtails.

Since she'd started talking, she no longer minded the nickname. Her little dimples winked. "Hi."

She'd been speaking more and more lately, mostly one-syllable words and one-word sentences. Still, Adam thrilled over every utterance. Jenny did, too. He could tell by her proud smile. Their gazes linked, and for one long moment, they were united by a shared joy.

"I told Abby what happened last night, and explained that I'll be staying here for a few days," Jenny said. "She gave her okay."

His daughter nodded vigorously, her eyes bright with excitement.

She was as gone on Jenny as Adam. There was nothing much he could do about that, except make sure Abby understood that Jenny was her teacher, nothing more.

"Oh, and Silas called," Jenny went on. "First thing Monday, the men you recommended will start on the roof. So, how are the horses this morning?"

"All fed and out to pasture."

"And the cows?"

"They're doing okay, and so are the bulls." Adam turned

on the faucet and washed up. "Who's hungry?" he asked both Abby and Jenny.

"Me!" his daughter shouted.

Jenny frowned. "You don't have to cook me anything, Adam."

"We always end up with extra pancakes, so it's no trouble."

"All right, but only if you let me help. What can I do?"

"How about starting a fresh pot of coffee, then you can fry the bacon. Four strips for me, one for Abby, and as many as you want."

Jenny was already on her way to the fridge.

"How many pancakes do you want today, Abby?" he asked.

"Three."

"You got it. While Jenny and I start cooking, why don't you head for the powder room and wash up? Then you can set the table."

Adam tossed Jenny an apron, and Abby scampered off. The moment she was out of earshot, he cleared his throat. "I didn't... I understand that today will be hard for you. I'll go with you to the cottage if you like."

Looking puzzled, Jenny pulled on the bib apron and tied the sash behind her. Then her expression cleared. "You're talking about my father. I miss him a lot, but I'm okay. He taught me to be a survivor."

In that way, Adam and Jenny were alike. Both of them had suffered, and they'd both weathered tough times. He pulled two frying pans from under the stove, and set one on the counter for her.

"This is going to sound weird," she went on, "but last night I spoke to him. Even though he isn't around, talking somehow helped. Does that sound crazy?"

Adam shook his head. "I've done it myself a time or two."

She gave him a sympathetic look and laid strips of bacon

in the pan. "I can't imagine what it must have been like to lose your wife."

"What they say is true," he said. "Over time, the grief lessens." But not the guilt.

"I'm glad to know that, Adam. And I really am fine."

Regardless of what she said, today would be rough for her. She could use a shoulder to lean on.

"I'll still go with you. We'll have to wait until Drew and Megan get up, so they can keep an eye on Abby. How many pancakes do you want?"

SITTING AT THE KITCHEN TABLE, Jenny sipped coffee and spent a leisurely morning reading the paper. Shortly after breakfast, Adam's foreman had called, and Adam had been outside since, leaving Jenny to play with Abby. He returned shortly before eleven. Now the little girl was settled in the family room, coloring and watching cartoons.

"No sign of Drew and Megan yet?" Adam asked.

Jenny shook her head.

"Those two never seem to—"

"We're awake, and we can hear you," Megan sang out.

Arms around each other's waists, she and Drew entered the kitchen looking rested and relaxed.

Adam caught his brother up on the ranch doings and asked Megan to keep an eye on Abby. Then he nodded at Jenny. "Let's go."

"Sleeping in did wonders for Megan and Drew," Jenny said, buckling in.

"Sleep is the last thing on their minds." His mouth quirked as he started the truck. "They're still honeymooning."

"You mean—oh." That explained Megan's contented expression and Drew's lazy smile. Jenny envied the couple, who loved each other openly and seemed to share everything. She couldn't imagine feeling that free and fearless. Did they even know how lucky they were?

As the truck meandered up the long driveway, she stuck her head out her window. The air was cold, but the sun, weak as it was, felt glorious.

When she straightened and put up the window, she caught Adam watching her through hooded eyes.

"You must think I'm out of my mind for sticking my head out the window the day after a snowstorm, but I couldn't resist. We haven't seen the sun in days."

"You may as well—it won't last long."

"I've never been here in the daytime." She gestured at the rolling fields that seemed to go on forever, and the cattle and men working. "Does most of the ranch look like this?"

"Pretty much."

"It's beautiful, Adam."

His face registered surprise.

"Did I say something weird?"

"You're the only woman besides my mother who ever called this ranch beautiful."

"I'm sure Simone loved this place."

Adam shook his head. "The ranching lifestyle was too slow for her." He looked taken aback, as if he hadn't meant to share that comment.

"Didn't she teach at the high school? That makes life interesting."

"It wasn't enough. She missed Missoula and the university."

Jenny recalled the conversation at Barb's that first day in Saddlers Prairie. "Because she wanted to earn a graduate degree?" she guessed.

Adam's eyes narrowed a fraction. "Who told you that?"

"I don't remember, but I heard something about her father being a professor and that she was supposed to follow in his footsteps. Then she met the love of her life—you—and forgot all about grad school."

"You heard wrong."

About which part? Jenny wanted to ask, but Adam compressed his lips, signaling that the subject was closed.

As Adam drove up Pinto Road, Jenny was quiet. There was no telling how she'd react when she saw the cottage, but it wouldn't be good. Keeping a wary eye on her, he pulled into her driveway.

One look at the debris piled out front and the blue tarp shrouding the roof, and the color drained from her face. "It looks even worse in daylight," she said.

He braked to a stop and glanced at her lap, where her hands seemed to have a death grip on each other. "Sure you're up for this?"

"No, but it needs to be done." She opened the passenger door.

After shrugging out of his jacket, Adam met her at the truck bed. He handed her a plastic crate and grabbed a couple for himself.

"Watch where you walk," he cautioned as they crossed the littered yard.

Jenny handed him her crate, fished the key from her purse and unlocked the door. She pushed it open, but instead of heading inside, she hesitated on the threshold.

She swallowed loudly. "Dear God."

He gave her a brief, reassuring squeeze of the shoulder. "Whatever you need from me, ask."

"Thanks." She gave him a grateful look that made him glad he was there. "All right, I'm ready now."

"Are we looking for anything in particular?" he asked.

"Whatever can be salvaged."

He nodded and they picked their way over the soggy living-room carpeting.

"This carpet is totally trashed." Jenny bit her lip. "So are the sofa and armchair."

"Make sure you let Silas know. His insurance should pay to replace both."

"I will." She stopped and bent down. "Look—my painted gourd!" She carefully pulled what looked like a crimson bowl from under a shard of ceiling plaster. "It's a little scratched up, but at least it's still in one piece."

She looked so happy, that Adam couldn't help smiling. "That piece means a lot to you," he said.

Jenny nodded. "It's African. Becca—my sister—sent it two Christmases ago."

"I didn't know you had a sister."

"She's a year older than I am. We don't see each other often, but we keep in touch through Skype and email."

"And likes to travel to interesting places, huh?"

"Actually, she lives in Africa, and has for years. She's a zoologist, studying monkeys."

"Interesting career. That's a long way from home."

"I think that's the whole point."

A telling comment that sparked Adam's curiosity, but like him, Jenny didn't appreciate questions about her family. One more way they were alike. Any other woman would've pressed him for more about Simone than he'd revealed earlier, but Jenny hadn't. Adam had respected that, and intended to respect her privacy in the same way.

Cradling the gourd, she turned toward the door. "I'm not going to put this in the crate. I'll just set it in the truck and get rid of my jacket while I'm there. I'll be right back."

When she returned, Adam was brushing off several books he'd found on the coffee table. "These are damp, but still readable."

"My child development books!" Jenny looked as if she wanted to cry. "Thanks, Adam."

They found a few other salvageable items in the living room and packed them into a crate. Next, Jenny headed for the bedroom with Adam following.

Back when he and Jenny were fooling around on her sofa, he'd fantasized a lot about coming in here with her, but not like this.

As she had at the front door, she hesitated before entering. "On the drive home from Miss Graham's last night, I thought about how I'd curl up in bed with a good book when I got here." She glanced at Adam. "I'm so lucky I was out when this happened."

If she'd been in bed when the tree came down... Adam shuddered at the very thought. "Damned straight, you are," he said, his voice gruff with feeling.

"I should call Miss Graham later and let her know what happened. By the way, she's very happy about Abby."

Adam nodded. "Tell her hello, and thank her for referring us to Carla Jenson."

"I will." Jenny's gaze traveled the wreck of the room. "I don't even know where to start."

"Why don't I clear out what's left in your closet."

"Okay. Is there anything left in the dresser?"

"I think I got everything, but you might want to check."

Still embarrassed over getting caught with Jenny's lingerie this morning, Adam turned away. They worked in silence, Adam filling a crate with soggy shoes Jenny might want and a few odds and ends from a closet shelf. She checked the dresser drawers, then picked her way toward the bed.

"The closet's empty now," he said. "Take your time while I load these crates into the truck."

When he returned to the bedroom, Jenny was crouched

down near the bedside table, clutching a framed picture to her chest.

"What's that?" Adam asked.

"Something I was afraid I'd lost."

He offered her a hand up. In the midst of twigs and roofing debris, she showed him the photo. The glass was cracked, but the picture itself seemed fine.

The five-by-ten, black-and-white photo featured two little girls and a thirty-something male with a stocky build, a square jaw and sad eyes. Wearing shorts, T-shirts and sneakers, they stood on a dock, holding fishing poles and a line of good-size fish.

"Is that you, your sister and your dad?"

Jenny nodded. "It was late summer. My mother had died a few months earlier, and we'd, um, left Indiana and moved to Seattle. Dad rented a cabin on Mount Rainier."

Her voice quavered some before she clamped her mouth shut, fighting back tears.

Adam had thought she'd been born and raised in Seattle. He wanted to ask, but didn't want to pry. He pointed at the picture. "You were a skinny little thing," he said. "And look at that white-blond hair."

"I was barely seven," she said, her voice stronger now. "As soon as I hit puberty, the color darkened to light brown. I thought about dying it back to blond, but Dad wouldn't let me."

"I like it natural." And the way the ends almost brushed her shoulders, and the silky feel of the strands between his fingers. Her skin felt even softer.

He cleared his throat. "You and your sister don't look much alike. She's bigger boned, with a rounder face. She favors your dad."

Jenny said nothing, but Adam guessed that she looked

more like her mother. To resemble the woman who'd abused you had to be rough.

"My father has a good face," she said.

He nodded. "A kind face." One that showed a world of hurt.

"He was a wonderful man." Her voice broke.

Adam didn't stop to think, just pulled her into his arms. "I know, honey, I know." He smelled her flowery scent. Warmth from her body seeped into him. Fighting the fierce need to pull her tightly against his chest, he instead held her loosely and patted her back.

"I'm okay," she protested, but she stayed right where she was.

In his arms. *Where she belongs.*

The wayward thought had him frowning and ready to back away, fast. But this wasn't about him. She needed him, and he wasn't about to let his fear get in the way right now. "Sure you are." His thumb made soothing circles over her shoulder blade. "If you carry your dad in your heart, he'll always be with you."

Sniffling, Jenny pulled out of his arms. Dark lashes framed damp eyes the color of new prairie grass in the spring. They were the prettiest eyes he'd ever gazed into. He swiped a teardrop from her cheek.

"Is that how you feel about your loved ones who are gone?" she asked.

"My parents. Sometimes."

"Not Simone?" The surprise on her face was clearly evident.

"No."

"Because it hurts too much?"

In so many ways. The loss was bad enough. Throw in guilt and anger, and you ended up with a truckload of awful.

Adam squeezed the bridge of his nose. "That's not something I talk about."

"I know. We both have our baggage. All the same, I'm sorry, Adam."

"Yeah. Thanks."

Oddly, instead of feeling the usual self-hatred and pain, his heart was full and open. It'd been years since he'd felt Simone's presence, but he did now. He sensed that she was giving her approval of him and Jenny and whatever they shared.

"Adam?" Head angled, Jenny frowned. "Are you okay?"

"Actually, I am." Better than in a long time. Lighter, as if a weight had fallen off his back.

He didn't stop to wonder where the pain had gone or why it had suddenly disappeared, he simply marveled at the unfamiliar looseness in his chest and gut.

After gently extracting the photo from its damaged frame, he handed it to Jenny. "Ready to go?"

"I am. Thanks for coming with me, Adam. I know I said I could do it alone, but I'm awfully glad you're here."

Gratified and then some, he nodded. "If you don't mind, on the way back we'll make one more stop."

"WHERE ARE WE GOING?" Jenny asked as Adam started the truck.

"Spenser's. I need to pick up a few things. They also carry picture frames, so maybe you'll find a new one there."

"What a great idea. I should also get some space heaters for the classroom."

Adam had been as sweet this afternoon as he had last night, holding her when she needed him most and saying what she needed to hear. He'd even told her a few things about Simone. Best of all, he hadn't pressed Jenny about her own past. "I'm so glad you're my friend," she said.

Instead of replying, he nodded. On the drive to town, neither of them spoke, but unlike other times, this silence felt warm and comfortable. Mainly because, for some reason, he seemed easier in his own skin, much more relaxed than when they'd left the ranch a few hours earlier.

Megan had called him a good man, and Jenny whole-heartedly agreed. She counted herself lucky to know him, and luckier still for his friendship. She wouldn't think about her deeper feelings for him, feelings she could never let out. Nothing positive could come of that.

The lot in front of Spenser's was packed, and Adam ended up parking on the far side of the post office.

"It's crowded today," Jenny said. "I've never seen so many cars here."

"That's because we beef ranchers are flush with money from the sale of our cattle."

Inside, the place was bustling.

"I'll meet you at the checkout," Adam said, and walked off.

Having no idea where to find the picture frames, Jenny grabbed a cart and wheeled it straight for the counter, where Connie Volles was ringing up customers.

Connie gave Jenny a sympathetic look. "I heard about your cottage. I'm real sorry."

Suddenly at least half a dozen people gathered around Jenny, adding their condolences. Several offered rooms in their homes, including Donna, the waitress from Barb's. "I have a spare bedroom—if you get tired of staying with the Dawsons. Ha."

Everyone laughed as if Donna had just cracked a joke they were all in on. Did they somehow know that Jenny had feelings for Adam? Of course not. No one did.

Feigning nonchalance, she smiled. "If I overstay my welcome there, I'll definitely let you know. Connie, will you point me toward the space heaters and the picture frames?"

Some fifteen minutes later, Jenny returned to the counter with two compact space heaters, an attractive pewter frame, magazines for Megan, Drew and Mrs. Ames, an I Can Read! book for Abby and a packet of specialty coffee for Adam.

"Thank-you gifts for the Dawsons," she told Connie.

Connie was counting out Jenny's change when she grinned at someone over her shoulder. "Hello, Adam. Those are real pretty."

Jenny turned around to find him clutching a fat bouquet of colorful hothouse flowers.

After clearing his throat, he thrust them at her. "These are for you, in memory of your father."

Connie's hand went straight to her heart. "Aren't you the sweetest man," she murmured.

In total agreement, Jenny nodded. Her eyes filled, and her swelling heart felt as if it would expand right out of her chest.

No matter how she fought her feelings for Adam, they just kept growing.

"Thank you, Adam," she said.

Ears reddening, he nodded.

An hour later, she set the newly framed family photo on the dresser in the guest room. Beside it, she placed Adam's flowers in a vase Megan had provided.

Jenny kissed her index and middle fingers, then touched them to the image of her father. "I'm glad I can talk to you, Dad. I miss you, but as Adam says, I'll always carry you in my heart."

Chapter Eighteen

The rest of the weekend passed without a hitch. Megan drove Jenny all over the ranch and gave her a full tour. In turn, Jenny helped Megan with her chores, including brushing and feeding the horses, and cleaning the barn, tasks she actually enjoyed. She met the ranch foreman, a weathered, lanky man named Colin, and a good number of the ranch hands. She also spent time playing with Abby.

Thanks to a ranching emergency that involved a wayward calf who got tangled in barbed wire and a visit from the vet, Jenny didn't see Adam Saturday night. Sunday he was out the door before she woke up, and didn't come back until dinnertime.

When she *did* see him, they were never alone. Before, she'd have suspected he was avoiding her. However, now when they were together, he seemed relaxed and at ease. Watching TV with the family Sunday night, he even joked around with her, as a friend would. Monday night was the same.

Their relationship had definitely evolved into a comfortable friendship. Which, given her growing feelings for him, was less than satisfying, but for the best.

During dinner on Tuesday, Jenny shared the latest about the cottage. "Thanks to the decent weather we've had, Silas says the men should finish the roof sometime tomorrow, then they'll repair the walls. If all goes well, they can then paint. The new carpet should be installed by late Saturday. By Sunday I'll be able to move back."

His expression shuttered, Adam said, "I know you'll be glad to go home."

Yes and no. Every day Jenny stayed here, she fell more deeply for him, and she knew she should get as far away from him as possible. At the same time, she enjoyed spending extra time with both Abby and Megan. Drew was a great guy, and Mrs. Ames cooked like a dream. Jenny also loved the big, comfortable house, the horses and learning about the complicated and demanding workings of the cattle ranch.

Moving back to the quiet little cottage was going to feel lonely. She forced a smile. "You'll probably all be glad to get rid of me."

Abby shook her head. "Not me."

Lately she'd advanced to two-word sentences. Jenny was thrilled, and by the grins the family wore, they were, too.

"I'm with Abby," Megan said. "I love having you here. Drew does, too."

Megan's husband nodded. "I appreciate you helping my wife with the chores, and keeping her company."

To Jenny's disappointment, Adam said nothing. Friendship only went so far. He was no doubt tired of her company at dinner, and he probably wanted his bathroom back, too.

"Did Abby show you the form I sent home?" she asked him. "The one explaining that tomorrow a reporter from the *Billings Daily News* will visit school to interview the students and me? He'll be taking pictures, too, that he might print in the paper, and I need your okay."

Adam's face clearly said that he hadn't heard any of this, so she explained about how Miss Graham had recommended her to the reporter. "I read his other articles about one-room schools in other parts of the country, and they were good."

She'd been relieved to note that the reporter had done little delving into the featured teachers' backgrounds. "Ours will be his last story, and it will be in the paper a week from tomorrow."

"You bet I'll sign the form," Adam said, looking impressed. "That's pretty cool, huh, Abby?"

The little girl nodded.

"Just think, our houseguest will be a celebrity," Megan said. "We'll be saying, 'We knew her when she was a mere mortal.'"

Jenny laughed. "Not just me—Abby, and the rest of the class, too."

Abby wriggled in her seat, her excitement obvious. "I… ice cream," she said.

"Right on, kid." Drew high-fived her. "We're definitely taking you and Jenny out for ice cream."

RODNEY BISS, A TALL, graying male with a double chin and big belly, arrived a few hours before the end of the school day. After telling the students about his job at the paper and answering their questions, he interviewed them and snapped photos.

As the door shut behind the last of the students and several inquisitive parents, Jenny turned to him. "Thank you for your patience with the students. They really enjoyed this afternoon."

"So did I. They're great kids. Especially little Abby Dawson. Talking for the first time at age five. Imagine that."

Jenny had briefed him about Abby earlier, and was especially pleased at the little girl's growing interaction with her classmates. "It's pretty special," she said. "The one-room school is a very nurturing environment. What questions can I answer for you?"

"First, let's snap a few more photos of you at your desk. Just try to look natural."

Jenny sat down and pretended to grade a paper. Soon the reporter set his camera aside, pulled a chair over and sat down across from her.

"I'd like to get a little background information on you," he said. "You taught in the Seattle School District for seven years?"

"That's right."

"Why did you leave?"

It was a question she'd anticipated. "I wanted to try something new and challenging," she said, repeating the same story everyone in town knew. "And I'm so glad I did," she added, which was the truth. "So far this has been a very rewarding experience."

Both the teaching and everything else. Even if she couldn't share her true feelings with Adam, knowing him, being near him was enough. At least that's what she told herself. It had to be.

Rodney Biss narrowed his eyes. "Did you expect me to say something else?" she asked.

"You haven't mentioned your father. He was a school principal in Seattle. How did his death impact your decision to leave the bustling city where you lived most of your life and move to tiny Saddlers Prairie?"

The reporter had done his research, which made Jenny nervous. She hoped he hadn't dug any deeper into her history than her father's death. If so, she would refuse to let him run the article. But his other articles had glossed over any personal details of the featured teachers' lives, and she was sure this one would be no different.

Besides, her father's death was no secret. "He was a wonderful man, encouraging me to grow in my career," she said. "He would've approved of what I'm doing."

Anything to leave the past behind.

Biss's pen scribbled furiously across his legal pad. Thankfully the rest of the interview centered on the challenges of teaching eight grades in one room. Rodney Biss was friendly enough, and Jenny relaxed.

"One last question," he said. "Coming from a metropolitan city, living here must be quite a challenge. Will you be teaching in Saddlers Prairie again next year?"

"There have been challenges," Jenny replied. "But for the most part, living here has been a positive experience. As for next year, I haven't decided. But please don't mention that in the article. I'd rather you stick to what's happening in my classroom this year."

Busy jotting down notes, the reporter didn't respond.

An odd feeling shivered up her spine, a premonition that something bad would come of this. But Miss Graham knew Rodney Biss, so he must be all right.

Jenny shook off the feeling and stood. Her guest followed suit. At the door, he shook her hand.

"As I mentioned, the article will run a week from today," he said. "You can access the paper online, but we'll also send you a complimentary hard copy."

As Jenny didn't subscribe to the paper, she appreciated that. "I'll look forward to reading it."

On the drive back to the ranch, she thought about the interview, which overall had gone well. The Dawsons subscribed to the paper, and would probably see the article before she did.

She was only sorry she wouldn't be at their kitchen table to see their faces—especially when they read about Abby.

To Adam's dismay, on Saturday night, Jenny's last at the ranch, Abby decided she wanted to watch a movie and eat popcorn with them both. Just the three of them. Adam wasn't thrilled about that, and didn't want his daughter getting any ideas she shouldn't about him and her teacher. But Abby insisted and Jenny seemed okay with it, so he went along.

After the monthly book-club meeting this afternoon, Drew and Megan had left, driving to another town for an overnight stay. A rare night away, making Adam think they were being pretty obvious about wanting to give him alone time with Jenny.

A bad idea. He cared too much, wanted her too much. A week ago, she'd called him a friend. That was what she wanted, and for the past week he'd played the part, and played it well.

Even if doing so was killing him.

His daughter picked *How to Train Your Dragon,* a DVD she'd watched at least five times.

Adam sat in the lounger with his own bowl of popcorn, and left the sofa to Abby and Jenny.

They sat beside each other, nibbling and watching the movie.

Not Adam. Jenny was too distracting. Laughing, bending down to murmur something to Abby, she made it impossible for him to look away.

Man, he had it bad.

It was a good thing Abby was here, or he might act on his feelings and ruin things with Jenny.

Who'd have thought his little girl would be acting as chaperone? Adam shook his head.

By the time the movie ended, he'd had enough of sitting here, lusting for what he couldn't have. He shut off the TV and stood. "Time for bed, Abby."

"Okay, Daddy."

Daddy. That was new, and the word settled sweetly in his chest.

Jenny smiled, her eyes soft with understanding. The

moment almost felt as if she were his wife and Abby's mother, sharing this special joy.

Do not go there.

"Abby." Adam gestured his daughter toward the stairs.

"Wait!" She scampered to Jenny, who opened her arms.

"Good night, sweetie. I'm so proud of the way you're talking, and I had such fun watching the movie with you. Sleep well, okay?"

Adam hoped someone would.

He followed his daughter and tucked her in, then read all of two pages of the story she chose before her eyes drifted shut.

Instead of tiptoeing out, he stayed for a while, watching her sleep and debating whether to head back downstairs or hide in his room. Unfortunately, it was all of eight forty-five. Too early to turn in.

Downstairs again, he strode through the living room, toward the mudroom. At least that was the plan.

Jenny stood directly in his path.

"Adam?"

Wary, he eyed her. "Yeah?"

"You seem distant tonight. Are you upset about something?"

What he was, was crazy with wanting her. He shook his head.

"Where are you going?"

"I need to check on some things outside."

"But when you did that two hours ago, you said you were done until morning."

"Changed my mind."

"Oh. Now I understand." She did that sexy thing with her mouth, catching, then releasing her bottom lip between her teeth. "We're friends—you can tell me the truth, Adam. You want privacy. No problem, I'll just go upstairs and pack."

There it was, the *f* word. If he didn't leave right now, he'd kiss her—and ruin the friendship he'd worked so hard to maintain, the friendship Jenny wanted. "I don't need privacy," he growled. "I need to get out of here."

Chapter Nineteen

Openmouthed, Jenny watched Adam stride away. She'd obviously overstayed her welcome, so it was good that she planned to leave after breakfast tomorrow. Judging by Adam's behavior this evening, not a moment too soon.

Tonight the easiness between them, which she'd begun to take for granted, had suddenly vanished. Adam had grown more and more tense as the evening passed. As if the past week had never happened.

What with work on the ranch and Jenny being there, he hadn't seen a lot of Abby lately. No doubt he'd wanted time with her, just the two of them. Jenny hadn't realized she'd been playing the third wheel, cuddling with the little girl, when Adam likely wanted to.

The back door closed none too gently as if underlining her thoughts.

If only he'd said something. Weren't friends supposed to be honest with each other?

Not about to hang around, making things worse by waiting for answers, Jenny headed upstairs. As she moved toward the guest room, an unpleasant thought struck her—that she was mistaken about Adam, that they weren't friends after all.

She'd hidden her true feelings for him and accepted that he'd never care as deeply for her. Now he didn't really want her friendship, either.

Sick at heart, Jenny shut the door to her room. On autopilot, she moved to the closet and retrieved one of the crates Adam had used to cart her belongings here. Near the dresser, she set it down.

The flowers he'd given her a week ago still filled the vase and sat beside Jenny's family photo. After so many days, the petals had wilted and browned, and were ready for the trash.

Much like her and Adam's short-lived friendship.

Sniffling and feeling sorry for herself, she opened a drawer. She was pulling out sweaters and packing them into the crate when she ran out of steam. The rest could wait until morning.

Downstairs, she heard the back door close. Adam was back.

Sorrow filled her. Automatically she reached for the photo. She'd been talking to her father every day now and finding great comfort in doing so. Tonight she needed him more than ever.

Clutching the picture, she sank onto the rug.

"I'm in trouble, Dad. I've fallen in love with Adam Dawson. Unfortunately, he doesn't even want my friendship." A funny sound spilled from her throat, something between an ironic laugh and a sob.

"You and I both know that's probably a good thing for him and for me. But it hurts, Dad. It really, really hurts, and I—"

The knock on the door startled her.

"Jenny?" Adam called out.

Adam. Had he heard her talking to her father? Oh, God, she hoped not. She hugged the photo to her chest.

"Open the door," he said.

"I'd rather not."

"Fine, I'll let myself in."

As the door opened, Jenny stood and set the picture in the crate. She raised her trembling chin. "I'm sorry about tonight,

Adam. I didn't realize you wanted Abby to yourself until it was too late. I wish you'd told me."

"This isn't about Abby. What you said a few seconds ago… is it true?"

Then he *had* heard. There was no use lying. Jenny chafed her arms and let out a heavy breath. "I'm afraid so. But you don't have to worry—I don't expect anything from you."

She assumed he would leave. Instead he closed the door and turned the lock. "You never said one word."

"Because I know you don't want anything to develop between us. I thought you wanted to be friends. Now I know you don't even want that."

To Jenny's horror, her eyes filled with tears. Hastily she brushed them away.

Adam scrubbed his face. "Jenny, I—"

Not ready to hear his excuses or agreement, she went blindly on. "I never meant to fall in love with you, Adam. You know that. There are so many things I haven't told you, things I can't share, that make loving you wrong. But you've been so kind and good to me, and—"

"Will you for once be quiet?"

She snapped her mouth closed.

"You're wrong, Jenny," he said. "I have feelings for you. Strong feelings. I have for a long time. I thought you didn't care about *me* that way."

Not sure she'd heard right, Jenny shook her head. "You mean we both…"

"Just come here." Adam pulled her into his arms.

FINALLY KNOWING HOW Jenny felt, Adam did what he'd wanted to do since the last time she'd been in his arms. Holding nothing back, he kissed her, a long, deep kiss that led to another and another, each one more passionate. It wasn't nearly enough.

From mouth to thigh, she molded herself to him.

Hungry to join with her, he backed her toward the bed. He pivoted away to yank off the bedspread.

When he turned again to Jenny, her top was gone. She was wearing one of the skimpy lace bras he'd stuffed into his pocket—pale pink and not exactly see-through, yet thin enough to show the peaks of her proud, rosy nipples.

Adam growled. Reverently he cupped each breast in his hands. "You are so beautiful."

Eyes closed, Jenny sighed. Moments later, she reached for the top button of Adam's shirt. "I want to see you, too."

She undid the buttons, her knuckles bumping his chest, her breathing as rapid as a sprinter's.

Impatient, he pushed her hands away and finished the job himself.

He reached for the snap on her jeans and jerked the zipper down. "I'm going to make love to you now," he said.

"If you don't, I swear, I'll burst into flames. Only…" She hesitated.

No matter how badly he wanted her, if she had doubts… Adam lifted his hands from her waistband. "You're not ready."

"Oh, I definitely am, but maybe we should talk first. There are things you don't know about me—who I really am. I wasn't going to ever tell you, but now…it's only fair that you know before we go too far."

Adam couldn't imagine what she meant. "I know you're a good woman who loves me and my daughter and cares about the ranch. That's all I need to know."

Unable to keep his hands off her, he leaned down and tasted her breast through the lace, gently suckling each nipple in turn.

She let out a throaty moan. "I can't think when you…" She broke off with a strangled breath. "You'll probably…

When you know everything, you might change your mind about me."

Distracted by her womanly scent and her petal-soft skin, he had no idea what she was talking about. And he didn't care. He forced himself to focus. "Nothing will change my mind, Jenny. There are also things I need to tell you. We definitely need to talk. Just not right now."

He returned to the pleasurable task of making her wriggle and moan.

A short while later, she pushed him away. "Do you have protection?"

"In my bureau drawer."

"Go get some, and hurry back."

Adam returned in record time and tossed a handful of condoms on the bedside table.

Moments later they were both naked, facing each other on the bed.

SKIN AGAINST SKIN WITH Adam—was there anything more sensuous? Jenny gave herself up to the pleasure. The smell of aftershave and Adam himself, the slick slide of his tongue against hers. His hair, short and bristly against her fingers. His thick lashes tickling her skin as he kissed her.

There was nothing and no one but Adam, filling her world with his hands, his mouth and his body.

He made love to her breasts, doing things to her nipples that drove her wild. She was already wet between her legs, aching for him there. Any second, she would climax.

"Adam, please." She lifted her hips, silently begging him.

"Patience, Jenny. I'm not through up here."

He caught her nipple between his lips and whirled his tongue around the sensitive tip, making her crazy with need.

Finally, when she was frantic and about to lose her mind,

he parted her sex and put his mouth and hands where she most craved his attention.

She shattered.

When she came back to earth, Adam was leaning on his elbow, a pleased grin on his face.

Jenny raised her eyebrows. "You look happy."

"I like pleasuring you."

She glanced at his jutting erection and gave a smile of her own. "Now it's your turn."

She'd barely circled him with her lips when he pushed her away. "I'm about to lose control. For that, I want to be inside you."

He turned away and sheathed himself. Jenny opened her arms, and he covered her with his body. Wrapping her thighs around his hips, she welcomed him inside.

In one thrust, he filled her.

Heaven.

"You feel so damn good," he said, echoing her own thoughts. Briefly he smiled into her eyes.

Jenny gripped his buttocks in her hands. "Love me, Adam."

He pushed in deep, then pulled back, almost leaving her. And again, and once more. Low in Jenny's belly, tension coiled tighter and tighter, bringing her to the brink.

Suddenly Adam let out a low moan. Thrusting harder, deeper, faster, he called Jenny's name. Pulling her with him into an explosive climax.

Afterward, they clung to each other, Jenny resting her hand on his chest, Adam cupping her hip. He reached up and turned off the bedside table lamp, plunging the room into darkness.

Her heart was too full to hold her feelings inside. "I love you, Adam Dawson," she whispered.

Adam kissed her tenderly. She tasted her essence on his lips. "I love you, too, Jenny."

Sacred, precious words. But would he feel the same way when she told him about her mother's schizophrenia? Because she had to tell him.

But needing to and doing so were two different things.

By the time Jenny mustered her courage, Adam's breathing had evened out. He'd fallen asleep.

Having risen before dawn and worked all day, he needed his rest. Besides, once he knew about her mother, his feelings would probably change. This could be Jenny's only chance to fall asleep beside him.

The truth could wait.

Her pricking conscience mollified, she, too, fell asleep.

Sometime later, Adam woke her with a passionate kiss. They made love again, slowly and sweetly. Not long after that, he sat up. "As much as I'd like to lie here with you all day, I'd best shower and start on those chores."

Jenny didn't want to ask, but she knew she was going to have to tell him about her family sooner or later. "I'll be leaving right after breakfast since my place is finished. When are we going to talk, Adam?"

"Abby's going to that Halloween party at Emily Spenser's Monday night—she's real excited about that, too."

Jenny felt his smile in the darkness.

"After I drop her off, I'll come over to your place. We'll talk then."

He kissed her tenderly. Then he was gone.

Chapter Twenty

The windless, star-studded night was perfect for Halloween, but at odds with Adam's churning gut. He'd never shared the truth about him and Simone with anyone. The thought of telling Jenny scared the hell out of him, but if he wanted a future with her—and he did—he needed to be straight about his marriage and his role in Simone's death.

"Your aunt Megan will pick you up after the party," he told Abby, who was dressed in a furry brown bunny costume, with whiskers painted on her face.

In the rearview mirror, she gave him a surprised look, her long bunny ears flopping comically.

"I'm going to Miss Wyler's house," he explained. "She and I need to talk." His voice cracked on *talk,* which just went to show how nervous he was.

Abby shot him a worried glance. "About me?"

"Not this time, ladybug. Miss Wyler and I both agree that you're doing great. Don't you think so?"

"Yes!" His daughter flashed a toothy smile. A moment later, she asked, "What, then?"

Adam wasn't sure how to answer. As much as he enjoyed Abby's growing ease at talking, at the moment he wished she couldn't ask. But she deserved to know. Hell, he'd told Drew and Megan—never mind that they'd already guessed.

Though there was no traffic on the dark, narrow road that led to the Spensers', Adam signaled and pulled over.

He turned around to face Abby. "Miss Wyler and I…" He cleared his throat. "We like each other. A lot."

"I know that."

It was the first time he'd heard her string three words together, and the first time he realized just how smart she was. "You do, huh?"

Abby nodded.

"How do you feel about Miss Wyler and me being together?"

"Happy."

She giggled, and Adam grinned. "All right, let's get you to that party."

A few minutes later, he walked her through the Spensers' front door. He greeted everyone and stuck around long enough to see Abby join in the fun. Then he left and sped toward Jenny's.

He'd last seen her at breakfast yesterday, not even forty-eight hours ago. It felt like forever. On the drive, he jumped back and forth between eagerness to be with her and uneasiness about the conversation ahead. By the time he parked the truck beside her car, he was all worked up, but also ready to share his past and move on. God and Jenny willing.

As he strode across the lawn, her front door opened.

"Hi, Adam." In the biting cold, her breath puffed out in a cloud. She tried to smile, but ended up with a pinched, scared look.

That she was nervous, too, didn't settle him down one bit.

His hunger for her was stronger, and the second he stepped into the house, he kicked the door shut and pulled her into a kiss. "I've missed you."

Jenny hesitated a moment, then wrapped her arms around

his neck for a long, passionate kiss that had him burning to get her naked. But things needed to be said.

Reluctantly he let her go, then glanced around at the freshly painted ceiling and walls, the carpeting and the new sofa and armchair. "This place looks great."

"Doesn't it?" She'd made coffee, and disappeared into the kitchen to fill him a mug. "Did you take pictures of Abby in her costume? Did she seem shy and anxious when you dropped her off tonight?" she asked when she returned with two mugs. She didn't usually drink coffee at night, and Adam wondered if she expected to be up late. He knew plenty of ways to keep her awake that had nothing to do with caffeine.

"Before we left the house, Megan snapped some photos, and I'm sure she'll forward them to you. Abby wasn't nervous at all. She joined right in, like those kids have always been her friends." Remembering how excited his little girl had looked, he smiled.

"That's wonderful, Adam. I'm so happy for her."

He nodded. "I told her about us." He set his mug on the knotty-pine coffee table, which had survived the roofing fiasco, then sank onto the sofa. "Drew and Megan, too. Funny, they'd all figured it out already."

"Maybe you shouldn't have said anything."

Well that wasn't the pleased reaction he expected. While he was still absorbing Jenny's words, she took the armchair across from him, instead of joining him on the sofa.

One day apart and she was already hesitant about their relationship—and he hadn't even told her about Simone. Adam's chest tightened painfully. "You didn't mean what you said the other night."

"Of course I did!"

He blew out a relieved breath.

"It's just…" Biting her lip, she fiddled with the sleeve of

her sweater. "After we talk, *you* might change *your* mind about me. You might not want an 'us.'"

"That goes both ways," he said. Jenny looked confused, but soon enough, she'd understand. Adam ran his damp palms over his thighs. "Megan's offered to pick up Abby after the Halloween party. That way you and I will have time to say everything that needs to be said."

He swore Jenny paled. During the next few tense moments neither of them spoke.

Feeling as if he might explode if he didn't get his story off his chest, Adam shifted on the sofa. "Mind if I go first?"

With a sigh of relief, she sat back. "Not at all."

"This is between you and me—no one else. Agreed?" He waited for her nod, then cut straight to the bone. "I haven't been completely honest about Simone. Her death is my fault."

Afraid of what he'd see in her eyes, he studied a callus on his palm, but he heard Jenny's sharp inhale. "Our marriage was wrong from the start," he admitted. "We didn't want the same things. Simone dreamed of life as a professor, researching and publishing. Ranching is in my blood—it's all I ever wanted. I belong here in Saddlers Prairie, on the land my family has owned for generations. Because we wanted different things, we argued all the time."

His throat raw from his confession, Adam paused for a sip of coffee. The brew tasted as bitter as his memories. "A few months into our marriage she started talking about a divorce," he went on. "Even though we were both miserable, I didn't want that. I was sure that a baby would bring us together and save our marriage. That's how I convinced her to get pregnant. If I hadn't talked her into getting pregnant, she could have had the chemo. She'd be alive today." After a beat of silence, he scrubbed his hand over his face. "So, you see, Simone's death was my fault."

As bad as explaining his sorry story was, telling Jenny

lightened the heaviness in his chest. Ready to face the condemnation he deserved, he raised his eyes and met her gaze square on.

To his surprise, he saw tenderness instead.

"You're wrong, Adam. You didn't cause Simone's death." She rose to her feet and rounded the table.

The warm, forgiving expression was almost too much to bear. "Don't you get it?" he barked. "My selfishness killed her."

Jenny didn't so much as flinch at his raised voice, she just sat down beside him. "But then you wouldn't have Abby."

"Yeah, I know." Adam squeezed the bridge of his nose. "But knowing Simone had to die…"

"You tried to save your marriage. I don't blame you for doing that. No one would. Not even Simone."

With dawning awareness, Adam realized she was right.

"Holding on to the guilt won't change anything. It's time to let go and forgive yourself." Jenny kissed his cheek, then offered her hand.

Adam grasped it, hard. She was right—he felt that in his gut. He was blessed to have found her, and her love and support meant everything.

Too overcome to tell her, he settled for a gruff, "You're the first person I've trusted enough to tell."

"Thank you for that."

Relieved that his story was no longer holding him back and that Jenny seemed to understand, Adam relaxed. He put his arm around her, and she settled against him.

For several long moments, they were both silent, Adam sipping coffee, Jenny leaving hers untouched. He was about to ask what she was thinking, when she sighed and shook her head.

"All this time, I got the impression you and Simone were the perfect couple."

"We wanted to be. It just didn't work out that way." He tightened his arm around Jenny's shoulders, then nuzzled her neck.

Jenny batted him away. "We're not through talking. I have skeletons of my own that I need to share."

"I'm listening."

Only he wasn't. He was kissing the sensitive crook where her neck and collarbone met.

Moaning, she angled her head for better access. "I can't concentrate when you do that."

"So don't. Just enjoy."

"But I need to tell you—"

He brushed his thumbs over her nipples, and she broke off with a gasp.

"And you will, honey. But right now, all I can think about is trying out your bed."

As JENNY DROVE TOWARD school early the next morning, a light snow sprinkled the windshield. She barely noticed. Last night Adam had stayed until the wee hours of the morning. One more night of unforgettable lovemaking.

And one more night without explaining about her mother's mental illness. She should've told him, but she'd lost her nerve, had let Adam distract her with his kisses. She'd buried her pricking conscience under passion and love.

Now, in the gloomy darkness of the cloud-laden morning, guilt smacked her hard, making her sick to her stomach.

Adam trusted her. He deserved to know. She *had* to tell him.

Even if it meant losing him.

Tonight, she promised herself. No excuses.

By the time she parked in the school lot, the wind had kicked up, the snow swirling furiously around her. In the short time between exiting the car and dashing inside, she was covered in the stuff.

She was shivering before the baseboard and space heaters and trying to clear her mind for the day ahead when her cell phone rang.

Adam, she thought. But Barb was on the line.

"The weather folks are forecasting a blizzard," the mayor said. "We're closing the school. The parents are being notified now."

"But I'm already here," Jenny said. "The roads aren't bad at all."

"They will be. Go home now, while you can."

Jenny hadn't even thought to bring boots. "All right. Thanks for letting me know, Barb."

"Before you go, did you see today's *Billings Daily News?*"

"No, I don't subscribe. Why?"

"The article about you and the Saddlers Prairie School came out this morning."

"A day early! The reporter promised to send me a copy, so I'm sure I'll see it soon."

"I had no idea about your mother, Jenny."

"My mother?" Jenny sank onto the corner of her desk.

"Schizophrenia and suicide—such a tragedy. That must've been very painful for you and the rest of your family."

"The reporter wrote about that?"

The horror and shock from the day a similar article had appeared in the Seattle paper roared back. Jenny covered her eyes with her hand. *Dear God, no.*

"I'm so sorry." Barb sounded genuinely sympathetic.

While Jenny was still reeling from the news, the mayor delivered one more zinger. "I'm also sorry you won't be teaching here next year. Everyone likes you. We thought you liked us."

"I do," Jenny said. "I haven't made up my mind yet."

"That's not what the reporter wrote. But, at least we know now, so we can start looking for your replacement."

If Barb had seen the paper, then so had Adam.

He'd learned about her family from a newspaper, just as Rob had. Adam was probably thinking she'd led him on, since she hadn't been sure if she was staying. He must be worried that Abby would be hurt—the very thing he and Jenny most wanted to avoid.

Suddenly Jenny had to see him. She jumped up. "Don't do that just yet, Barb. We need to talk about this, but can it wait until later? I need to find Adam."

If the mayor was surprised, she didn't let on. "Of course."

Within seconds, Jenny shut off the heat, locked up and started the car.

The snow was falling harder now. A blanket of white covered the prairie and was beginning to stick to the road. A situation that called for careful driving, but Jenny needed to find Adam.

Throwing caution to the wind, she stepped on the accelerator, pushing the car to high speeds. After a dangerous slide that scared her half to death and almost nosed the car into the steep ditch lining the highway, she eased off. But her heart continued to race, and by the time she turned into the driveway to the ranch, she was desperate to reach Adam.

Near the back door, she screeched to a halt. Heedless of the snow seeping into her loafers, she rushed from the car. Slipping and sliding, she made her way to the porch and up the steps. After a quick rap on the door, she let herself in through the mudroom.

Mrs. Ames was at the sink. The folded newspaper lay prominently on the kitchen table, impossible to ignore.

The older woman's eyes widened. "Why, Jenny. I didn't expect you this morning. Megan just phoned. She and Abby were on the way to school, but the mayor announced the closure and they turned back."

Bracing for condemnation and hoping Abby knew nothing about the story, Jenny nodded at the paper. "Did you see the article?"

"Wasn't it supposed to be in tomorrow's paper? I haven't had time to even scan the front page, but I will now."

"Please don't." Jenny snatched the paper from the table. "I need to find Adam."

Mrs. Ames gave her an odd look, then shrugged. "He and Drew are over at the annexed property, herding the cattle toward the most sheltered pastures while they still can. With this weather, you'll want to take one of the Jeeps. The keys are in the barn. First, though, take off those shoes and put on some boots."

"I will—thank you."

After quickly trading her loafers for boots, Jenny raced out. While waiting for the engine to warm, she flipped through the newspaper to find the article. With shaking hands, she skimmed through it.

There were several quotes from her students and a few cute photos. One featured Abby. The first part of the article was filled with good information about the school. A few paragraphs later, just as Barb had said, Rodney Biss had spelled out Jenny's entire family history. Then adding insult to injury, he misquoted her, making her sound ungrateful and unhappy with the school and Saddlers Prairie. Hot tears filled her eyes.

Her cell rang. Phylinda Graham was calling. Jenny knew she had to talk to her and would explain everything—later. She let the call go to voice mail.

Five interminable minutes later, visibility narrowing as the snow flew fast and furious, she slid sideways across the snow-slick ground, braking to a stop mere yards from Adam, Drew and several of their crew.

Adam looked surprised to see her. Snow coated his hair and shoulders. "What are you doing here in this weather?"

"School's closed, and I needed to talk to you."

He frowned. "Now?"

"Now."

"I'll be back," he told Drew and his men.

Jenny led him to the Jeep. In the short time since she'd turned off the engine, snow had covered the windshield, blanketing the car in darkness and privacy.

"What's this about?" Adam asked.

"Did you read today's *Billings Daily News?*" she asked.

Frowning, he shook his head. "With the blizzard coming and so much to do, I didn't have time. Why?"

Relief flooded her, followed by real fear. In a few minutes, she would know whether he still wanted to be with her or not.

"The article on the school came out early." She passed the folded paper to him.

"That's great, honey." He set it aside. "I'll read it later."

Jenny shook her head. "You need to look at it now."

"Can it at least wait till we get the cattle squared away?"

"No." She nodded at the article.

Curiosity was etched all over his face. "All right, then."

Dreading his reaction, she gnawed her thumbnail while he read.

When he finished, he silently passed the paper back to her. Jenny couldn't tell what he was thinking.

"Now you know everything I wanted to tell you the other night," she said.

"Did you know the reporter was going to write all this stuff?"

She shook her head. "He never even hinted that my background was important to the story." Afraid she might cry before she said what she needed to, she hurried on. "If you want to break things off, I understand. It won't be the first time."

Adam gave her a sideways look. "What exactly are you saying, Jenny?"

"Shortly after my father died, a similar story came out in the Seattle paper. Not long after Rob read it, he broke off our engagement."

"Why'd he do that?"

"Because I hadn't told him about my mother. You see, her illness hurt and embarrassed my family so much." Now that Jenny had started, she couldn't seem to stop. She hugged herself, the words pouring out. "Dad wanted to erase the pain. Even when our mother was alive, he never allowed my sister or me to talk about how she acted. Then after she died, we moved out to Seattle. No one ever mentioned her again. Dad's motto was, Bury the Past and Move On." Which Jenny now knew didn't work.

"Like she never existed," Adam said. "That, of course, made her bigger than life."

Jenny gaped at him. "How did you know?"

"Because I did the same thing after Simone died. Go on."

"My Seattle friends and colleagues and Rob all knew that my mother had died when I was little, but nothing beyond that. Then they all read the story in the paper and learned about her illness. I never dreamed that information would be printed for all to see. Rob was really upset that I hadn't told him."

"I hear that."

Adam wouldn't look at her, he just stared at the snow-shrouded windshield.

The chill inside Jenny had nothing to do with the weather. She tucked her icy fingers under her arms. "Rob was frightened, too. Schizophrenia can be genetic. When it is, it often skips generations. Becca and I don't have it, but if either of us has a child... I have bad genes, Adam." Jenny swallowed. "I should've told Rob, and I should've told you."

"So why *didn't* you tell me?"

"I was scared. After people found out in Seattle, they distanced themselves from me. That hurt. The real reason I came here was to escape my past." She gestured at the article and let out a bitter laugh. "That sure backfired."

"Maybe the people in Seattle treated you differently because you didn't trust them enough to tell the truth. You didn't trust them to forgive you for lying, either."

Jenny had never considered that.

Adam crossed his arms. "That's why you didn't want a relationship with me—because of your mother and the schizophrenia?"

Jenny nodded. "But I fell in love with you, anyway. And yet I still hid the truth about my past from you. I'm so sorry I hurt you, Adam. And sorry for any pain my lies might cause Abby."

Weighed down with regret and heartache, she wanted to crumple into a ball and cry. Instead, she raised her chin. "Thank you for listening. I know you need to get back to work, so I understand that you can't keep talking. I'm going to head back to the cottage." She started the Jeep and cranked up the wipers.

"Have you looked outside? You can't go anywhere. I'm sure as hell not letting you drive, especially off the ranch." As if seconding the statement, the wind suddenly gusted, shaking the car. "Trade places with me and I'll drive you back to the house."

She thought about arguing with him, but he was right. Driving in this weather would be foolish. Besides, Adam was already out the door, his head bowed against the stiff wind and snow.

Scooting across the space between the seats, she moved into the passenger seat. Seconds later, he started the car.

With visibility a scant foot or so, Jenny couldn't see Drew or the other men. She thought she saw the lights from the other two Jeeps and heard the roar of their engines. "Did Drew and the crew finish with the cattle?" she asked Adam.

"I think so." Adam inched the Jeep slowly through the blizzard. Intensely focused on driving, he was silent. Or maybe he was simply through talking to her.

Jenny couldn't blame him. She was too empty and numb to worry about the weather, her cold feet or getting herself home.

Adam didn't speak again until he pulled up beside her car. Leaving the heat on full blast, he turned to her. "I don't care about your mother or your genes. I love you, Jenny."

They were words she'd never again expected or hoped to hear. "Are you sure?" she asked, searching his face.

Without a moment's hesitation, he nodded. "I am."

"But what about children? Don't you want more?"

"I won't lie to you—I do. We'll deal with the problem together. We'll get genetic counseling. Then, if you're afraid to have kids together, we'll adopt."

His generosity and love awed Jenny. Her heart was so full of love, her eyes filled with tears. "Adam Dawson, I love you."

"You'd damn well better. Now, let's go inside."

Arm in arm, they lowered their heads against the wind and started for the house.

Just then, Drew and Colin and the other crew members pulled up next to them.

As soon as they exited their Jeeps, Adam raised his voice over the howling wind. "I have good news. Jenny Wyler loves me."

Drew and the rest of the men hooted and whooped. Adam grinned, and she laughed.

In the mudroom, they hung up their coats and slipped off their boots. They headed into the kitchen. Mrs. Ames was making cocoa. Abby and Megan sat at the table.

"I heard about the article," Megan said, "and I told Mrs. Ames."

The housekeeper nodded.

Glancing at the people she cared deeply for, Jenny bit her lip. "I should've told you all. I'm sorry."

"No harm done," Mrs. Ames said. "You're still the same woman."

Megan nodded. "We don't care about your mother, we care about *you*."

"We like you," Abby said.

"The part about my mother was true, but some of the other things in the article were totally false." Jenny reached for Adam's hand.

He eyed her. "What about the part that says you're only here until the end of the school year?"

Jenny smiled at the man she loved. "Completely untrue. I wouldn't dream of leaving."

Epilogue

Eight Months Later

Gazing at her reflection in the bathroom mirror at the community center, Jenny hardly recognized herself. "I look so different in a gown and all this makeup," she said. "And my hair! Anita did a great job."

Her sister Becca, who'd flown in five days earlier, sniffled and nodded. "You're gorgeous. I just wish Dad could see this."

Mrs. Ames sighed. "You make a lovely bride. Come here, dear, and let Megan and me help with your veil."

Moments later, Becca and the other two women nodded, pleased with the results.

"You look beautiful," Abby said.

"Thank you, sweetie." Jenny admired her soon-to-be daughter's lilac-colored dress, frilly socks and white patent-leather Mary Janes. "So do you."

"Adam will flip out when he sees you," Megan murmured. "I think we're ready. Mrs. Ames, would you please let the musicians know?"

"Will do. See you out there." The housekeeper cast a fond smile at Jenny, then slipped through the bathroom door.

Becca squeezed Jenny's hand. "I'll be out there, proudly watching both you and Abby."

Overcome with emotion that her sister was here to share this special day, Jenny bit her lip and nodded.

Abby watched while Jenny and Megan freshened their lipstick. She was unusually quiet. Jenny turned toward her slowly so as not to wrinkle anything. "You're not your normal chatty self this afternoon. Is everything okay?"

With eyes that were huge, the little girl nodded. "I want to look just like you when I get married, Mama."

Mama. Abby had been using the name since school had let out a week earlier. Jenny still wasn't used to the name, but whenever Abby uttered it, she melted.

"You're already so smart and pretty, Abby. When you get married someday, you'll make a beautiful bride."

"Megan?" Drew called out, then knocked at the bathroom door.

"Don't come in!" she shrieked.

"Okay, but it's time."

As if on cue, the quartet, four musicians from a nearby junior college, struck up the interlude music.

"Ready?" Megan asked.

Jenny nodded.

"See you in a few." Megan slipped out to join Drew as best man and matron of honor.

As they disappeared into the auditorium, Jenny nodded to Abby. "Okay, sweetie. Your turn."

With a solemn nod, Abby retrieved the straw basket filled with rose petals from the counter, then followed her aunt and uncle.

Moments later, the music changed to what she and Adam had chosen for the bridal entrance.

Jenny pulled the veil over her face. "Here I go, Dad," she said. "I've found the love of my life. He knows all my secrets, and I'll never keep another from him. Be happy for me."

Heart pounding, she swept slowly into the auditorium.

Gasps filled the packed room as everyone turned to watch her walk down the aisle. For once, she enjoyed being the center of attention.

She passed her beaming sister, students and their parents, Val and Silas, Barb and Emilio, Phylinda Graham and Carla Jenson—the friends and acquaintances she'd come to know and care about in this wonderful community.

At the front of the room, Adam waited with the minister.

He looked so handsome in a tux. His eyes were bright with feeling, and Jenny knew he liked her dress. He smiled, and she forgot everyone else.

As she floated toward her husband-to-be, she knew she was exactly where she belonged.

* * * * *

HEART & HOME

Heartwarming romances where love can
happen right when you least expect it.

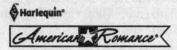

COMING NEXT MONTH
AVAILABLE MARCH 13, 2012

#1393 COWBOY SAM'S QUADRUPLETS
Callahan Cowboys
Tina Leonard

#1394 THE RELUCTANT TEXAS RANCHER
Legends of Laramie County
Cathy Gillen Thacker

#1395 COLORADO FIREMAN
Creature Comforts
C.C. Coburn

#1396 COWBOY TO THE RESCUE
The Teagues of Texas
Trish Milburn

REQUEST YOUR FREE BOOKS!
2 FREE NOVELS PLUS 2 FREE GIFTS!

 Harlequin®

 American ★ Romance®

LOVE, HOME & HAPPINESS

YES! Please send me 2 FREE Harlequin® American Romance® novels and my 2 FREE gifts (gifts are worth about $10). After receiving them, if I don't wish to receive any more books, I can return the shipping statement marked "cancel." If I don't cancel, I will receive 4 brand-new novels every month and be billed just $4.49 per book in the U.S. or $5.24 per book in Canada. That's a saving of at least 14% off the cover price! It's quite a bargain! Shipping and handling is just 50¢ per book in the U.S. and 75¢ per book in Canada.* I understand that accepting the 2 free books and gifts places me under no obligation to buy anything. I can always return a shipment and cancel at any time. Even if I never buy another book, the two free books and gifts are mine to keep forever.

154/354 HDN FEP2

Name	(PLEASE PRINT)	
Address		Apt. #
City	State/Prov.	Zip/Postal Code

Signature (if under 18, a parent or guardian must sign)

Mail to the **Reader Service:**
IN U.S.A.: P.O. Box 1867, Buffalo, NY 14240-1867
IN CANADA: P.O. Box 609, Fort Erie, Ontario L2A 5X3

Not valid for current subscribers to Harlequin American Romance books.

Want to try two free books from another line?
Call 1-800-873-8635 or visit www.ReaderService.com.

* Terms and prices subject to change without notice. Prices do not include applicable taxes. Sales tax applicable in N.Y. Canadian residents will be charged applicable taxes. Offer not valid in Quebec. This offer is limited to one order per household. All orders subject to credit approval. Credit or debit balances in a customer's account(s) may be offset by any other outstanding balance owed by or to the customer. Please allow 4 to 6 weeks for delivery. Offer available while quantities last.

Your Privacy—The Reader Service is committed to protecting your privacy. Our Privacy Policy is available online at www.ReaderService.com or upon request from the Reader Service.

We make a portion of our mailing list available to reputable third parties that offer products we believe may interest you. If you prefer that we not exchange your name with third parties, or if you wish to clarify or modify your communication preferences, please visit us at www.ReaderService.com/consumerschoice or write to us at Reader Service Preference Service, P.O. Box 9062, Buffalo, NY 14269. Include your complete name and address.

HARI1B

New York Times *and* USA TODAY *bestselling author*
Maya Banks presents book three in her miniseries
PREGNANCY & PASSION.

TEMPTED BY HER INNOCENT KISS

Available March 2012 from Harlequin Desire!

There came a time in a man's life when he knew he was
well and truly caught. Devon Carter stared down at the dia-
mond ring nestled in velvet and acknowledged that this was
one such time. He snapped the lid closed and shoved the
box into the breast pocket of his suit.

He had two choices. He could marry Ashley Copeland
and fulfill his goal of merging his company with Copeland
Hotels, thus creating the largest, most exclusive line of re-
sorts in the world, or he could refuse and lose it all.

Put in that light, there wasn't much he could do except
pop the question.

The doorman to his Manhattan high-rise apartment hurried to open the door as Devon strode toward the street.
He took a deep breath before ducking into his car, and the
driver pulled into traffic.

Tonight was the night. All of his careful wooing, the
countless dinners, kisses that started brief and casual and
became more breathless—all a lead-up to tonight. Tonight
his seduction of Ashley Copeland would be complete, and
then he'd ask her to marry him.

He shook his head as the absurdity of the situation hit
him for the hundredth time. Personally, he thought William
Copeland was crazy for forcing his daughter down Devon's
throat.

Ashley was a sweet enough girl, but Devon had no desire

to marry anyone.

William had other plans. He'd told Devon that Ashley had no head for the family business. She was too softhearted, too naive. So he'd made Ashley part of the deal. The catch? Ashley wasn't to know of it. Which meant Devon was stuck playing stupid games.

Ashley was supposed to think this was a grand love match. She was a starry-eyed woman who preferred her animal-rescue foundation over board meetings, charts and financials for Copeland Hotels.

If she ever found out the truth, she wouldn't take it well.

And hell, he couldn't blame her.

But no matter the reason for his proposal, before the night was over, she'd have no doubts that she belonged to him.

What will happen when Devon marries Ashley?
Find out in Maya Banks's passionate new novel
TEMPTED BY HER INNOCENT KISS
Available March 2012 from Harlequin Desire!